THE MAN WHO LOVED PLANTS

Edgar Oliver

THE *MAN* WHO LOVED PLANTS

PANTHER BOOKS
New York

Manufactured in the United States of America
First published as Panther Book No. 2 in 2004

Library of Congress Control Number: 2003106252
ISBN: 0-9708476-2-9

Cover painting by Helen Oliver Adelson,
photographed by Harvey Adelson
Back cover photograph by Ludovic Fremaux
Proofread by Micaela Porta
Edited by Romy Ashby and Typeset by Foxy Kidd

Panther Books is an imprint of
Goodie Publications
197 Seventh Avenue 4C
New York, NY 10011
www.goodie.org

Special thanks to the Golda Foundation and Harry Blevins.

I

The train station was so large as to contain its own weather — a weather of high marble walls that held the same chill in winter and in summer — the weather of a concrete vault so massive as to have become the sky, beneath whose distant, dim-lit curve a fog seemed to gather. Above all, it was the weather of echoes — all sounds hollowed and shattered so that words got lost and yet continued sounding long after those who spoke them had taken their trains and gone.

Above the colonnade that buttressed these marble walls, at the point where the concrete vault launched into the void, giant stone warriors encircled the waiting room. They stood at intervals, naked, staring sternly ahead. Each warrior held a shield in front of his sex.

A boy sat in the curving belly of a bench in a far corner of the waiting room. He was surrounded by piles of luggage — battered suitcases stuffed to the point of bursting, shopping bags, portfolios, and bundles held together by rope. His posture was so languorous that the curve of his frail body echoed the curve of the bench's belly with the exactitude of liquid. His legs seemed to be flowing, spilling over the bench's lip. He might have been a large rag doll, inanimate as the suitcases that surrounded him, but for the intermittent flitting of his ponderous eyes and something that hinted at breath in the parting of his lips.

His was a strange face. Looking at it, one might have felt no one had seen this face before and that, having looked away, still no one would have seen it. It both denied perception and compelled observation. Behind the incongruous curves of that face, both tender and antique, something mournful receded.

He did not move. But his eyes roamed about the waiting room, always flitting back to the door marked "Ladies' Room" whenever it swung open. This door was of giant height and cast of solid bronze, but it seemed to swing effortlessly on its hinges. Even infants who could barely walk could push it open. The door swung in to reveal a fluorescent cavern of white tile and massive wash basins. Mirrors reflected other walls of tile that receded into the distance.

This shard of room vibrated painfully before the boy's eyes for a moment. Then with a sigh of suction the door glided shut. The bronze panels sealed against their marble frame with a quiet yet portentous clang that echoed of the door's enormous weight.

The rapidity with which the door sucked itself shut, the sigh it emitted, and this finite clang all began to seem malign to the boy. No one ever pushed the door beyond a certain point, so all he saw was a thin shard of the bathroom — never enough to make out the room's shape nor where in its depths the toilet stalls were hidden.

Strangely, no one ever used the wash basins or the mirrors that were visible in the narrow scope of the door's opening. Perhaps the ladies were too shy of being seen primping, and only used the mirrors farther back in the bathroom's unknown depths. Every now and then he caught glimpses of the reflected backs of ladies' heads peering into mirrors. He kept hoping the next opening of the door would reveal his Mother coming out, or that he would at least see her putting on her makeup at the mirror. She could put it on as slowly as she liked, just so long as he could see her there doing it. It seemed to him that she had been in the Ladies' Room an awfully long time.

He didn't know how long ago she had gone in. It had seemed then such a simple thing, he hadn't given it much thought — nor whether she had looked back at him strangely before the door shut behind her. But he began to imagine she had. The waiting room clock was broken and he could not abandon their luggage to look for another clock. No one came close enough for him to ask the time. His voice was not strong enough to carry and, besides, he had never in his life voluntarily spoken to a stranger.

He looked up at the rows of giant naked soldiers and wished their shields would fall away. He had never seen a grown man naked, in flesh or photograph. It did not occur to him that he could ever hope to attain, to possess in his own body the physical perfection of these warriors. Yet in some nebulous and unadmitted way he desired to possess them — to possess or to worship.

It began to seem less important to him how long ago his Mother had gone in than how long ago the fear had come over him that she would not return. From where had this fear come, and why? Why would his Mother abandon him like this? Had she truly been in the Ladies' Room so long he must accept the fact that she was never coming back or was dead? Was there another exit, a window she might have crawled out of? She had taken her pocket book — that mysterious and bottomless receptacle of all important objects — with her. But that was natural.

For a long time the fear was so vertiginous and painful it precluded all thought — even these futile questionings and suppositions. The fear moved faster and faster like a giant thing rushing toward him, or his own frail being in the throes of a nightmare of speed accelerating toward an unknown void. The fear made time itself whir — so that the time of her absence passed faster and faster, leading to greater and greater fear of her no return.

Never had so many throngs of travelers, the shattered prongs of their laughter and conversation clashing about the room, rushed away through the exit doors leading to the tracks. They moved so quickly they seemed to move against their will — as though the void beyond that battery of doors were a great orifice of suction inhaling this stupidly laughing crowd, sucking them into a giant funnel of time and departure. The strident timbre of their laughter was harsh and derisive. It made of this constantly shifting crowd a malign cohort to the giant will to acceleration that annihilated them even as they threw themselves into its jaws with mocking laughter.

They seemed to be mocking him. Their laughter was directed toward his own paralysis and fear. With one shriek he could have stopped it — caused the giant sucking lung beyond the doors and its endless throng of victims to deflate — fall still and shattered to the stone floor while one last shard of laughter brained itself against the ceiling like a deranged bat and then fell echoless with a china clink atop the whole dead pile.

But he could no more have uttered this shriek than he could have stood and walked over to that door that barred him with one harmless word — "Ladies" — pushed it open and entered that vault of shining bone, that sanctuary that was now a vacant mausoleum where one tortuously questing word would wrench itself from his throat over and over — "Mother?"

She would be gone without a trace. But the comfort of this deadly knowledge would relieve him of his fear and hope. Yet he could not do this. He could not rise and walk through that door any more than he could have shrieked.

Eventually the last traveler was sucked through the doors into the dark realm of the tracks. "It had to reach an end," he thought. "Yet — how strange for it to have ended." The entire procreating chain of humanity, leapfrogging carelessly and derisively through time, had been sucked out and packed off toward its many destinations. Time began to move more slowly. Now, rather than fear and acceleration, the excruciating slowness and solidity of time became unbearable to him.

Time lay reflected across the vacant and shining expanse of marble floor. Time exfoliated from the cornices and vaults, the arches and columns in wide, slow-blooming sheaths of fungus. These sheaths grew heavy with their breadth — the expanse of silent and eternal simultaneity. They dropped and settled on the floor, stacking up in weighty layers while new sheaths of fungus bloomed from the ceiling to replace them.

Distant clangs and intermittent screeches of metallic friction were the painful death cries of any possible willed action. Layers of decaying time stacked themselves up to his chin, then above his head — so that he breathed a different air, saw through a thicker, slower substance. The fumes generated by this decay pulsed out in bubbles of nothingness.

Balloons of vacuum clasped by thin, cold skins bobbed randomly about the room — unpoppable and yet at times bouncing against him with a terrifying, engulfing elasticity.

The bronze door to the Ladies' Room was now sealed shut by the very weight of time that demarcated the heavy substance of the waiting room from the stabbing and fluorescent hum behind that door.

Behind that door on the tile floor lay the cold, empty, and invigorating pang of the last vainglorious action ever committed — his Mother's abandonment of him. There remained for him only one fear, one hope — that the huge decaying carcass of time, eternally dying in its sleep, would roll over and crush him unwittingly beneath its steel-shanked belly.

Even as he feared and hoped for this annihilation, he knew the stone warriors would not permit it. Staring out sternly at the beast of time that could not touch them, they waited for its slightest quickening against him. Then their shields would fall away and they would spring to save him. But what weapons lay hidden by those chaste shields that could quell the wrath of time? Their stone sexes, raised quivering in defiance, were the only weapons they could flaunt against the weight of this all-consuming, crushing beast.

When night fell, though, he could smell the night, feel its cold fingers snaking through the labyrinth of this, his marble tomb. Though he could not see the night he smelled it, felt the stirring of it, its weightlessness, smelled its toplessness — acrid smoke of star and moon and purple nothingness rushing, falling away, pouring eternally out from the earth to fill the exposed void.

This was the first night of his trance. It came cold to him and in sorrow to touch him with its distance. He might have gone mad. Any other boy would have who, so shy and afraid, was paralyzed and unable to question his fate. But he had always loved sorrow and had considered it his fate, and sorrowing his most noble yearning, since his earliest memory of the huge, odorous, and ancient world.

So he wrapped himself in the trance of melancholy and sorrowed through the unknowable time of his trance.

How he could have thought of himself during that time it would be hard to say — but he could hardly have considered himself human.

Rather he was a repository for sorrow, a sanctuary for its sweet, slow unfoldings. Locked in his fragile stillness that could so easily have been broken, the night air came to him and the odors of the seasons and of shuddering day came with offerings to his sorrow.

In the day rays of light falling from the vault revolved, stirring up a breeze that shriveled the black fungus and blew it away. Time became no more than a perfume, a sweet odor from the fanning of the light that stirred all things.

A shafted pain skewered and stiffened him. As the pain grew it seemed unbearable. But at its ultimate pitch it hardened and grew cold like a thing of iron, and he grew used to it. This pain bolted him to the bench. It seemed to him in his lack of corporeal awareness that he had grown into the bench, become part of it — a sheath of being as invisible and thin as the reflections that lived in the hollow of this wooden basin and gave it depth.

He no longer looked at the door to the Ladies' Room. But he began to create in his mind the scenario of his Mother's death. Not that he thought she was dead. He was just compelled to imagine her death, over and over. Sometimes the details would shift, or he would linger over them differently — but the basic story remained the same.

His Mother had just risen from the toilet, like a nymph from the waters. Yet she was encumbered by her clothing, manacled, made vulnerable by it. Her skirt was hiked about her hips and, below her girdle, her sex was visible. A pearl of urine clung to the soft hair adorning her sex. A fragment of tissue, almost like a feather, clung there as well, seeming to tickle the dark parting of her vulva's lips. Then the other woman appeared.

From where she had come, how she had entered the confines of the stall, he could never tell. Nor could he tell what she looked like. All he could see clearly were her hands — as a person who has gone for years without a mirror might raise his own hands to his face and picture himself as his hands. Her hands were white and lovely, with long, red lacquered nails. But the nails were hard and sharp as talons, and the purpose of these hands was vengeful and cruel. They ripped open the top to his Mother's dress, revealing her bosom.

His Mother's breasts heaved with the shock of rape. The other woman's hands attacked — viciously, gleefully. The sharp red fingernails clawed into his Mother's breasts, mutilating them. Her nipples seemed to struggle. But the sharp red nails closed in on them, scratching and pinching, twisting and severing them. His Mother struggled silently but her sex cried out. The hands attacked her sex. He could make each tortuous second of this drama last as long as he wished — could speed it up, slow it down, freeze the whole struggle and go back in time to refine some erotic detail he had overlooked, then put the attack in motion again. His eyes always floated somewhere near the attacking hands, so that his view was both detailed and shiftingly disembodied.

The hands were flawlessly white, seemingly immune to the blood they drew. The shiny red nails dug into his Mother's sex, sank into the ripe flesh of the pubis as though it were made of butter. Then the slim fingers parted his Mother's sex and slid into it. The hand clenched again and the nails clawed her from within and from without, twisting and mutilating. His Mother sank to the ground glassy-eyed as the blood flowed from her.

As he imagined this scene he lapsed into an erotic frenzy, silent and still, his eyes closed — but no less aroused than if he were writhing and gasping. The erotic shuddering was clasped within his mind. His entrails, had they shuddered, were so thin they would have made no more than a ripple in the dim light of the waiting room.

He created and imagined this scene of his Mother's death compulsively. But he by no means always thought of it. Most of the time, thoughtless, he was a sensor for ecstatic shifts in the weather — long unseen by him but nonetheless reaching him on the crawlings of the air. The child he was still wandered about somewhere, lost but no longer subject to the walled-up weeping of lost children — quietened, quelled, subject to the smell of earth. He was not shocked or ashamed by the hideous intricacies of his erotic imaginings. He thought of himself as pure — suffering from a purity that approached the nature of cruel things.

He had fallen back into the center of his spiral — unreachable, hovering at the very wellspring of his being, as thin as his own breath and barely able to contain it. It almost did not matter whether he ever moved again or not.

II

At some point the image of his Mother's death began to grow less compelling, less arousing. He imagined it less. The stone warriors began to hold erotic sway over his mind.

They existed for him in a countryside of rock that channeled many streams and led them astray, never letting the streams conjoin or reach an end. The rocks hummed with the pent-up force of the streams and unleashed odors of labyrinthine wetness. Harsh and leafless trees clung to the rocks. Purplish buds sprouted from their jagged branches. These buds were secret and compelling. Held quivering within themselves, they never burst.

Sometimes a single warrior stood in this countryside, as still and naked as the rocks around him. Spray from the streams chilled his flesh, still and cold as stone. But his eyes were lustrous and hot. Searching the horizon of this countryside of chasms, they seemed to defy yet yearn for approach.

The boy would approach and begin gauging with his hands the girth and strength of the soldier's limbs — as though gauging the strength of a tree or a face of rock he was about to climb. Though he longed to, he never dared kneel and slip his arms behind the shield so he could clasp the soldier round his thighs and feel his heart pound against their unyielding mass. Finally, slowly, the soldier would notice him, as though withdrawing unwillingly from a trance.

From the soldier he never dared imagine a passionate or urgent touch. But lowering his shield and lying down on the rocky earth with a silent and sorrowing passivity, the soldier would spread his thighs like a river god and allow the boy to feed from the wellspring of his compulsion. The boy would impale his throat on this weaponry — so massive and unyielding as to be insensate. The only response he ever got from the soldier was an increase in the strain with which his breath tried to rip the two nipple-pointed muscles of his breast apart — and the strange rotation of the psyche as, quietly and at a distance (always seen from below in the boy's crouching posture of subservience), his eyes closed and his lips parted.

At other times the soldiers were many, and seemed intent on destroying one another. There was no rhyme or reason to this battle conducted across the rocky countryside. No reason perhaps other than the boy's desire to watch them destroy one another. In fact, they existed to be one another's enemies — and it would have been hard to tell friend from foe as, oftentimes, they all looked exactly alike, absolute replicas of one another. At times two of them would gang up in some detailed scenario of combat against a third. But as soon as he was dead, the two supposed allies would engage in their own fight to the death.

These writhing battles could continue for hours until once again only one soldier remained. Surrounded by the corpses of his brethren he stood at attention, his shield held before him, and stared off stern and unyielding into the distance.

During the throes of combat and of death these writhing bodies strained to their utmost and attained a beauty unnoticed by the combatants themselves. Weaponless, their only means of killing were strangulation and drowning, both of which demanded a reclining posture. The victor crouched lengthwise over the writhing body of his victim. The drowning warrior's head was hidden by the waters of the stream. But every part of his body seemed imbued with its own soul and life and to struggle hopelessly against its own death. Especially the warrior's sex, held jutting toward the sky as he struggled for his last breath, seemed to die its own death.

At times the only difference between the stone warriors and their living selves was the life he imagined within them. They could stand for days entranced, ignoring one another. He could never fathom this — their obliviousness to one another. He wanted to scream, "Are you blind? Are you mad? How can you resist one another?" Almost in a rage of impotence, he could not imagine why the vaulted heavens above him did not echo with the groans and sweats of their ecstatic couplings — almost as violent as their slaughters of one another. Yet they never touched one another with desire, or even looked at one another except with intent to kill.

Between and behind these recitations of torture and desire — the odor of the earth held him in remembrance of a self that could be swallowed by the long, slow mounting of the stairs in that house of rotting and disjointed perspectives, that leaky wooden house cast adrift on mud puddles whose cold depths clenched the roots of the surrounding trees and held them up, that house where a century separated one room from another, the staircase was its own dank century, and looking out the window one could be swallowed for a century by the heaving of the guardian trees that brooded for more rain.

III

One day he stood up and, filled with an almost forgotten sense of urgency, walked over to the door of the Ladies' Room, pushed it open, and went in.

The room's emptiness seemed to deny his existence. The room was a vast cube of white tile, as high as it was wide. At the center of the ceiling a huge fan dangled from a chain. The fan's rotation was sluggish. It hardly stirred the air. But those long, slow-turning blades filled the air with expectation. On every side he was surrounded by washbasins almost as broad as tubs. Their white underbellies resembled the swollen throats of enormous frogs. The mirrors reflected only one another. Bars of fluorescence flanked the mirrors. The hum given off by these shafts of light, rising in pitch imperceptibly toward eternity, became confused with the whirring of the fan and with his own entrails — so that he felt this whole vault of mirrored bone humming in his guts.

A narrow opening was cut away in the center of the room's far wall. This cleft that split the wall all the way up to the ceiling sank away in a narrow passage flanked on either side by doors to toilet stalls. At the far end of the passage, almost hidden by shadow, he saw a window.

Slowly, his heart rising in his throat to the fevered pitch of the fluorescent lights, he moved toward the cleft in the wall. The doors to all the stalls seemed to hang slightly ajar, as though tempting entry. But he could not be sure. The perspective was confusing. The hall seemed to sink steeply upward, so that the window at its end seemed at the top of an unscalably steep shaft. He could not be sure each door was ajar until he came abreast of it.

He pushed each freely swinging door inward — first to his right, then to his left. Each door reverberated against the interior wall and swung back, not coming to rest until he had advanced a few doors beyond it. But in these brief, wide yawnings he had time to gauge with a sweeping glance each stall's emptiness. The regimented similarity between each stall, their glistening, repetitive spotlessness began to pain him. Though what, if anything, he hoped to find he did not consider. This pristine barren repetition, each battery of chrome conch shells stuffed with fat toilet rolls of equal girth that never dangled beyond a certain point — the complete lack of stain or odor — seemed to deny from the start any trace or clue of human passage. Only now and then a toilet gurgled away, trickling monotonously into itself. As he approached the end of the line, he was benumbed by the hollowness of an empty tomb.

The window hung before him — a last resort, a last, frantic possibility. Yet he did not rush up to it, for it was impossible from the start — blocked by a row of thick iron bars firmly anchored into the wall of its recess. Not even the thinnest child could have slipped between them.

Slowly he moved to the window and with his almost strengthless hands tried to shake the bars. He could not wring from them even a hint of weakness. Feeling no strength left, he clung to the bars and held himself up by them. He cupped his forehead into the narrow opening between two bars and looked out the window.

It was night. The window looked onto an alleyway paved with bricks. The window where he stood seemed to form the dead end of the alley. It led away into the distance. Here and there jutting flanks of buildings, ill-defined in the light, forced the alley to veer so that eventually it veered out of sight. These buildings seemed dislocated, asymmetrical, as though their stone flanks had been eaten away from verticality by the settlings of time. No windows were alight in them.

But light filtered from unseen street lamps through narrow passages between the buildings and here and there picked out some weathered intricacy of stone scrollwork. Where this light fell to the ground, each brick it fell on was both blood-dark and silver — the shadowed niche between each brick incredibly sharp and black. A prong of sky, a frozen bolt of lightning, hung above him. The stars there looked cold and cruelly distant. He stuck his arm between the bars and held it out as far as he could. The air was chill and moved in a slow, steady breeze like a current in broad water. The smell of the air was so moving to him he could barely breathe. It brought home to him that for an uncounted time the only smells to reach him had crawled eternally on the settlings of the air until they snaked into the vault where he sat still. Rumors of traffic and laughter filled the night. And from around some corner the tidal flashing of a neon light washed the stones and bricks with purple and red and made them shine with wetness.

His Mother had walked down that alley. There could be no other possibility but that she had. He saw her, a shadow except where her silhouette crossed the silver puddles from the street lamps. Yet how recognizable her back! She carried her pocketbook as she always did — slung in the crook of her elbow — so that her hand was cupped in a Chinese gesture across her belly.

This intimately imagined detail — his Mother's hand, invisible yet so clearly seen — had for him the pang of clarity of a vision from long ago. She moved catlike beneath her clothing, following the fascination of her senses open to the night. When she reached the chasm flooded by the beating of the neon light she stopped and turned back her head. Her eyes would have met his, standing at the window, but she had already disappeared round that narrow corner a long time ago.

He too wanted to walk down that alley, turn that corner. The craving was so powerful that, unconsciously, he wounded the bones of his hands against the bars at the window. It was not so much to find his Mother or to follow her that he craved to walk down that alley. Rather he felt the same desire and fascination she had felt — his nostrils leading him on to consume all the unknown air that flows in a night. And he recognized this alley as the magic passage into the night — the street that led where no other street could, the mysteries round whose narrow corners might remain forever hidden, unattainable, if hunted from another street.

He raced back down the passage toward the cathedral of wash-basins and the bronze door. But before he reached it he remembered the pain in his entrails. He went into the first toilet stall and stood there for a moment examining the clear water that quivered slightly in ringlets in the porcelain basin. As he unzipped his trousers he began to shudder, and the hair on the back of his neck prickled. He took one long ecstatic gulp of air and then the ray of steaming urine shot from him. It jutted from him in a rod that indented the waters of the toilet and made them boil. It seemed to him that his entire body leaned against this liquid rod and that in the strength of its focused speed it held him up. He leaned there for a long time, and for what seemed decades this gushing rod did not bend beneath his weight or deviate into the weakening of an arc. He expulsed the decades in a focused rod of time's green and yellow, brilliant, gushing waste. And the weight of decades, of centuries was lifted from him. His being inflated with vigor and with youth — and the husk of ancience that had held him crumbled and washed away along with all the pain of his antiquity.

But in that fatal moment from which there is no forgetting or returning, unwittingly in his innocent ecstasy he fingered himself and found in that heretofore unconcerned and carefree tropic of his body a lush growth of hair. As the pain of his antiquity fell from him a new pain was born with this discovery, this unhoped-for unearthing of the sorrow between his legs. This pain would never leave him — sorrow sprung whole and vigorous in a night, it seemed.

When he emerged into the zone of mirrors, he looked at himself. A growth of beard clouded his chin, and above the skeletal jutting of his cheeks his eyes rose high, wide and dark as liquid planets whose gravity he could not resist until he tore himself from them and, stumbling through the bronze door, headed for the rumor of the streets — not looking once at the bench where he had sat or the stone warriors who had guarded him so long.

Day, not night, took him on the broad palm of her gold discus hurled slanting through the rising of the spring air. And he was hurled away over the broad discus of the earth that stretched the fabric of the city almost to breaking with the warmth of its exhalations.

He never found the alley, for the night of its finding was gone. To return to it, he would have had to return to the fluorescent hum of the Ladies' Room and the bars of the window atop the steep shaft of night — and he could not bring himself to do that. He moved painfully in outgrown clothes. But he did not mind the pain in the ecstasy of motion and eventually, falling prey to the softness of a hill, he lay down in the grass and wrapped himself in the smell of weeds and gold.

IV

Go back. Go back. How could you have imagined yourself then? As a creature more conceivable, more possible than the hero you are inventing now? Hardly — for you were impossible, an impossibility — and to have lived on air alone for years would be simpler than to recapture from lost years the rigors of your ecstasy. How I wish I could go back to you, my impossible one, driven on like a wild animal by your nostrils into the inhuman zone of lost odors. More alone than I could ever describe you, you invented your own lovers and, though speechless with self-pity, did not pity yourself enough for what you were — a giant boy, half monster and half man, hideous, raw, and chaste.

V

There was this proud revulsion he felt at times — almost every day at one point or another. It was, among other emotions, one of the few most necessary to his survival. This revulsion would surge up in him at the sight of public schools, of buildings devoted to vocational training, employment offices, or any building devoted to the institutionalization of drudgery.

When eyed with shock or disbelief by the shifting hordes of six o'clock's workaday homeward flux, he would raise his head high in scorn and walk as a prince, while at the same time biting back the tears of self-consciousness. This revulsion was not prideful of itself but was necessary armor to cloak his complete inability to take part in the functionings of humanity. He would not have known how, or whom, to ask for work. Had the thought occurred to him, the words, barely conceived in his mind, would have stuck in his throat to the point of choking him.

Even more powerful than scorn to drive him into the unreachable outskirts of his isolation was an almost insane self-consciousness. Having no inkling himself of what he was, he could not bear for others to rest their eyes on him. If looked at by a stranger — and there were nothing but strangers — an awkward monstrosity bloomed within him and he fled like an accursed beast.

This self-consciousness gave him the inexhaustible energy of desperate and unceasing roaming. He would never have sat down on a doorstoop for more than a few minutes except on the most deserted of streets. Thus, during the first few weeks of that spring of his return to life he was driven to roam unceasingly — to the point where it seemed that he survived on motion and that the act of walking was all that was necessary to sustain the life within him.

During the course of this one endless walk he collected loose coins, and even bills, he found on the street. He hoarded this small treasure and used it sparingly — at rare intervals going into large supermarkets to make small purchases and shoplift. It was not surprising he was so adept at this. His supreme and terrified self-consciousness found in this thievery a perfect complement, for shoplifting was of its very nature an act of invisibility.

He would take his booty to the cemetery or the park. They were close to one another and were both so large that in their depths the city fell away behind the crests of the trees and ceased to exist. Both the cemetery and the park contained many forgotten stretches where no one came. Only in those places where he was completely isolated would he sit down to eat and, afterwards, to sleep.

These were the only places he rested — except in the hush of public libraries where he would sometimes read voraciously all day, for some reason only the works of dead authors. He clove to the events and passions of these lives now dust to such an extreme that, being unbelievably thin, he could slip in between the pages of a book and close the cover over himself. In this way he lived many lives but never spoke. His own life held no events except this endless walk and wandering — driven forward by an unknown desire, feeding on his own motion until, driven by hunger to brave the terrors, less of thieving than of the token purchase, he pocketed his illegal feast and returned to the cemetery or the park.

Sometimes he would not leave their confines for days and became himself a tree — a tree moving among trees, ecstatic to their stillness and sparsity of gesture. He was rarely perceived among the trees, though sometimes he did watch people from a distance. If by chance a wanderer there or an amorous couple reclining on the grass made out his eyes bent on them through the shadows of the foliage — those two burning, disembodied things trapped within a face so gone to leaf as to be invisible in the underbrush so frightened them that they stood hurriedly and ran off.

VI

Had I known that I was made for this
no time could have bereft me of my childhood.
Or if time gave me no choice
I would have refused its treachery
and stayed longer to smell out the cold
in the backyard when the rain lured
        me to abandon
until, having turned to stone,
I had stayed too long.
But things pull back from abandon,
and dying was always easier then
        than now.
A monster finds a true mirror
        when he first yearns for a kiss
and says to it
"Had I known that I was made for this... "

VII

That city seemed to him ancient. Clouded by time he could not, never thought to hold it up to the memory of his childhood visit. The streets were full of mystery for him — a mystery that predated humanity, as though the people were the product of the streets and not the reverse. These buildings, rich with capacity for decay, had drawn their inhabitants as savages who, wandering there, had stayed to nest.

During the course of his walks he sometimes reached a point of mystery beyond which he did not yet wish to trespass — a curve in the street beyond which the ground rose, creating the impression that the land lay according to a different law — a high wall whose soft brick flank caught the leafy dappling of the light at a certain hour and to which he told himself he would return at that same hour in that same season but round which, for many years perhaps, he would not look — always preserving unexplored territories in which he would have the potential to be lost.

In other directions his explorations branched out for vast distances — into seemingly endless suburbs whose gleaming, already heat-wracked expanses pushed back the possibility of the city's edge into a dim, deluded hope for forests. At these times he grew frightened, feverish, and thirsty as in a desert of vehicular speed and turned back toward his park.

Each walk was an exaltation set out on with the possibility of no return — as though when approaching the crest of a hill beyond which the street seemed to drop off into a void, or sortying round that wall whose mystery he had not yet dared approach — some magic combination of circumstance, his feet trespassing in an occult stride some invisible boundary, might change the archings of their bones to something less human, lift him, launch him into an inconceivable landscape.

VIII

If sorrow could be eaten he would have grown fat. Yet the mountainous black lady who sat sagging her door stoop, sagging the patient grey wood of the threshold into a curve to cup her contented sitting, she was not sorrowful.

He sat in the small park and watched her on the sly. The park was a triangle, more like an extension of this rotting row of backyards that had become confused with it through the utter dilapidation of their fences. The few sickly trees in the park, thinner than his ankles, cast no shadow. He sat in the shadow of the buildings. Grey dust from the park's clay hide rose up on fitful breezes and sought the slanting liquid plane that separated the collapsing shadow of the buildings from the light. Settling, the dust seemed to settle only on the pigeons, bearing some ancient grievance against them. Nearsighted, they mistook bits of tin and broken glass for food. Their entrails jangled as they waddled.

Her yard was wet with the oozings from her kitchen window, as though the vast pots that steamed there salivated humid clouds of lust for mud pies. From time to time the dust of the park was sucked up in funneled clouds and swallowed by her zone of mud.

The whites of her eyes were more expressive than any form of human life he had ever seen. With a blue-yellow sheen like ivoried teacups, they demarcated the meanderings of her gaze, slow perhaps, but quick and unexpected couched within her massive stillness. How many years she had sat there it would be hard to say. The buildings sagged around her, were absorbed into her queenly stature. Nothing could be more content than slowly to consume the world with one's each abstracted, musing, smelling-more-than-thinking breath.

At any moment he expected her to rise onto her flattened feet and roll sideways off the wooden step into the oozings of her mud, letting out a bottomless roar of satisfaction as she wallowed in the wet earth. But she did not need to. She had a whole brood of children to do it for her.

Out they raced from the kitchen. Blocked by her girth in the door, they were forced to climb onto her shoulders and slide down her breasts, tumbling off her lap into the mud. Randomly she seized their heads as they scaled her and with her huge hands pressed their heads against her, chafing and rocking them. They nuzzled against her for a moment and another dust rose from the chafing of their skins, and a sound almost of slapping dough when her palms cupped them. It was as though they rode the surface of another planet, seized by her gravity. Their legs were thinner than her fingers and their flesh much darker, as though all the pigment within her had mellowed and dissipated through the years of her vast and ancient burgeoning into stillness. They were sharp and concentrated with bitter, questing movements, malicious in their harryings of one another. Girls and boys alike, they were all of the same tiny stature, frail as though hatched from a single egg. Were they her children or her grandchildren? What could possibly be the generative link between these thin, spritely creatures and herself?

He stood and continued his walk, while toying with the idea of asking her if he could live with her and be her servant. But she would not know what to do with a servant, and what words he could say to her he could not figure out.

The sky, with the incredible activity of spring, had all of a sudden knitted itself up into huge clouds, each one as big as a mountain. These clouds had not blown up from anywhere but had amassed themselves out of the nothingness of the sky. The clouds began to grow dark as the neighborhood shifted. He was now on a wide avenue of shops — ten cent stores, coffee shops, and discount centers — but everything was closed and no one was in sight. It must be Sunday.

Suddenly a huge wind filled the street and he knew the clouds were lowering. He smelled the approaching rain.

He walked into the rain and it surrounded him. He could go on walking forever, leaning into the wind, eyes almost closed against the rain's lashing.

Then a desperate fluttering made him turn his head. Through the rain, in a sheltered zone of shadow, he saw a photograph of a naked man. It hung before his eyes for a second and then was whipped away by a stream of other pages that turned more quickly than any human hand could turn them, more quickly than they could be seen, cracking like whips in the desperate wind. He stepped under the shelter of a magazine kiosk's awning. He was drawn imperiously by this magazine that hung agonizing in the wind — as though the wind, maliciously, turned the pages to tempt his eye, whipped them by so fast he could barely see them.

His fascination was so overpowering he did not care if the keeper of the newsstand saw him staring. One glance at her reassured him absolutely. She was obviously blind and had not heard him because of the violence of the rain beating on the awning. How he knew she was blind he could not have said — her eyes were hard and bright as billiard balls. They seemed to bear down on him with an absolute recognition too horrible for her to endure if she truly were seeing him.

Her lips were slightly parted. Out from between them, as though gushing directly from the depths of her brain, came a harsh, inhuman humming. This humming held no trace of melody, but a compulsive rhythm of silences, of gasps, punctuated it. He knew she thought she was alone and that if he made the slightest sound she would stop. At times the hum would sustain itself for impossible stretches, leaving her no time to gasp in more breath. At these times her noise became unbearable to him — liquid madness, spittle and vomit of her brain gushing from her lips. But he did not dare reveal his presence. And he could not move away — paralyzed by his desire. A hollow sickness invaded his entrails, rooted him before this magazine agonizing in the wind. He prayed that the wind would not die down and yet would come more slowly, leave each tantalizing page hung before his eyes so he could relish it and sicken himself further with desire.

One photograph in particular he longed to see again. A muscular and hair-clad man leaned back against a wall, his arms spread out against its rough surface, hands open palmed, the fingers curled in graceful passivity. In wonderment he gazed down at his own sex. It flourished silently beneath the rocky curve of his abdomen. Though unaroused, his sex seemed ready to explode with its own vigor. Yet it was tender and vulnerable in its sleep. His lips were moistened with a slight smile as sweet as the smile of a Madonna gazing at the baby Jesus.

He longed to see this photograph again. But the glimpses he got of it were briefer and briefer as the magazine was wrenched back and forth by the wind. It hung beyond his reach in the zone of forbidden publications. What separated it from him was less the money to buy it than the courage to pronounce its name. And what of she who sat beneath it, the blind one? She seemed to glory in the agony of these magazines she could never read or look at — as though the cracking and shuddering of their pages, almost like a scream that surrounded her, revealed to her their contents — and the humming, wordless scream that vomited from her head was the wind itself. Why was she sitting here in the rain, her kiosk open on a Sunday when there was no one to buy her candy or her publications? In the shadows the chamber behind her seemed to stretch not back but down, spiraling through the sidewalk toward a lightless hollow where, shrunken and alone in her black chamber without limits, the whites of her eyes would glow with the heat of her relentless thinking.

He turned away from her back into the rain. He now held this photograph clasped within his mind — more vividly than he could have ever seen it. The image moved within him, elaborating on itself, making stories. Sometimes he was the hand that touched, sometimes he was the sex, aroused by the compulsive force behind that foreign hand that moved and caressed — always he was himself, hollowed with desire to contain these images. Sometimes the hand was slow and tender. At other times its purpose was castration, and the blunt fingers clenched the scrotum mercilessly, while the sweet smile that moistened the curve of those musing lips was contorted by sudden agony. But always the hand moved with desire — and withdrawing as though to obliterate the fact that it had ever touched, left those lowered, half-seen eyes musing over that mystery, that other intelligence at the tropics of the torso, eternally separated as though by time itself from the hunger of those sweet, smiling lips.

As the rain stopped vast sheets of reflection coalesced across the ground. The sky hung upside down in the wet streets, and the pigeons reappeared, wheeling in it. He approached the train station.

In its hollow it was as though it had not yet rained. The warriors waited. He went into the Men's Room. Locked into the cubicle whose intimate darkness crouched beneath the high exposure of the marble vault, he lowered his trousers and for a moment saw his own sex suspended upside down in the waters of the toilet, like that other's sex suspended high above him that one day he might reach with his lips. Sorrowfully and intently he took himself with his hands. That image played itself over and over in his mind — and dissolved into other images as yet only half imagined, half imaginable. But he saw himself also, crouching in a solitude that also crouched, as though for a beheading — intent upon himself, curled back into himself, waiting.

When the flux unleashed his desire to die on the floor and he stooped to wipe it up, watching the white liquid mingle in the wad of tissue with the mud from his footprints — he thought in sorrow that perhaps for many years, perhaps forever if forever meant never until it was too late, this would be the solitary ritual of his desire.

He went to the row of basins and looked in the mirror. He was held fascinated by himself. He saw there a semblance of beauty. Yet, clouded by his beard, he could not remember his childhood face. The border of his lips was masked so that he could not tell their shape. And if he clasped his beard down with his hand and strained to look at himself three-quarters, a horrible vacancy he sensed about his chin hinted at some hidden ugliness. In the sorrow of no desire the thought came to him that his mouth was a wound and that hidden beneath his beard was something monstrous he might never have the courage to reveal — though in its unveiling there might be a strange and vengeful glory. He looked in his eyes and saw there the cruelty of all thought and, smiling to himself, was proud to think his smile was cruel. When someone came in he began to wash his hands as though he had not been standing there very long. As the water hit his fingers he felt along them tiny, frantic contractions — the death agony of his sperm.

IX

This is not the city as it was but the city as it was seen by him, a wanderer who did not wander there but rather through a landscape sprung from his own desire.

He was held in the contemplation of lowly things — discarded, disused objects — the rust running along the fence, running, forever running to the strength of its own current — the settling foundations of houses tortured away by time from their true shapes — the cool dirt creeping from under the sidewalk, weeds undermining with their roots, cracking the stone skein of the city. He loved such things.

Had he thought of himself in so many words, he would not have thought of himself as human. He thought of himself as the protector of the streets, almost a demi-god whose duty was to walk, conversing with the streets as he walked through them, appreciating, perceiving all the still, unuttered life within them — a life that had been lost in thought for centuries inside all lowly objects. Gone unseen and ignored for so long, it thought of leaving altogether, one day quietly unfolding its wings and flying away. But he would converse with it, make it stay — this thing gone mute and hidden, this life lost long ago.

Sometimes in the park the trees oppressed him — those objects of great beauty fulgurating, breathing the massive breath of their branches — a great tide swelling from them, the fire above the leaf turning the air to glass. They, even they reeked of death and seemed to fan it along, to speed it with the great wind they exhaled. The fire above the leaf burnt his eyes and robbed him of his breath. Lying down at the center of the great speeding bowl of day he looked at the trees that pained him with their silence and knew they mocked him — his puny being thrust toward annihilation so fast he would die without having spoken. And there was little to say to them anyway. The trees did not speak. Their knowledge was masked by severity of gesture.

Then perchance some godlike youth in running shorts would amble past thinking of the waxing of his car, his girlfriend, tennis. And he would rise, strung on the stave of desire like a top and follow hypnotized though at a distance — his eyes like madhouses yearning to incarcerate those flanks, those buttocks, thighs, that fleshy snail slung in the nylon sack. He had gone so long unspeaking and unspoken to, but for the mockery of children and of drunken brutes, that if not for these he might have thought himself invisible — these and the painful consciousness that he might be looked at.

X

He advanced into the idyllic zone of a shadowed and antiquated suburb long since wrapped round and held by the city. The old trees made their first full shadowings on the grass so green as to have been forgotten and remembered with a shock. The houses loomed behind their porches like huge and long-locked cabinets whose brooding contained chamber within chamber — the hollow spiraling of all the trees from which they were hewn. The breathing of lush bushes held up their broad steps and the skirtings of their ground floor windows.

He stopped. Nothing was deeper than the unknown depths of this house — nothing sharper than the gold edges of the leaves where the sun, still cold in its morning brilliance, cut round the corner of the shed to touch the bushes. The dirt gave forth frost and the wooden flank of the house was purple and gold in patches as the shadows of the foliage moved against it. Someone slept behind this wall and the wall held the music of his sleep.

"I could live in this house for years," he thought, "like an old lady in the emptiness of her over-ample home, drawing in the milk and bike-delivered groceries with a steel claw, then tossing a change purse out the mail slot — never seen, though peering out the windows. I would not question or rearrange the furniture, quilts, lace doilies, chests of mementoes, rockers mysteriously abandoned by that old lady

I would impersonate. But to be outside at this hour is to be immortal, older than the eaves of this house but younger than the birds that awake in their shadow."

As quietly as possible he moved away from the side of the house, round the jutting bay of its porch, and across the swell of the lawn back to the sidewalk. Here under the trees all was still purple. He moved secretly, hoping not to waken anyone. But already some people were awake, children especially, eager to be outside. He shied away from the children because they above all would stare at him flagrantly and mock him with words.

The street seemed miles long. At the end of the trees' tunneling he could see a place so far away as to be indecipherable, except that it looked to him like a wall of foliage that rose high, higher than any of these trees, and glowed green and gold like flames as it moved in the wind and sun.

At the end of the shadowed street this burning wall of leaves and light looked like it might be the entrance to another world — the final passage where the city fell away into an unknown wilderness. He moved slowly toward this flaming point at the end of the tunnel, hoping it was not an illusion, believing in its gold savagery. Each house he passed, ample and high, skirted with porches and brooding up into the trees, was mysterious to him. He could be a child again if left alone in any one of them — when the weather was older, the shadows darker, and not even his Mother knew what was hidden in the cabinets and chests of drawers, locked in the unused bedrooms and looming in the closets.

As he approached the end of the tunnel of trees and the wall of leaves rose brighter and higher, the sharp and awesome smell of dawn, faster than a flock of birds and quieter, rose from the earth and vanished. In the backwash of its departure he halted almost in fear. Then, like a hot wave rolling from the South thunderously over the backyards, almost melting and flattening the chain link fences and making the heads of small trees swing like pendulums, the smell of summer rolled in with a shock. It was a smell compounded of the boiling of air inside parked cars, the melting of vinyl slipcovers and flip flops, the droning of lawn mowers beheading grass, fat white burgeoning of roots, and generations of gnats born and died in a puddle.

This smell, almost a raging noise, was crazed in its aseasonal intensity — like a tidal wave of time overlapping itself, all summers yet to come consumed by the jealousy of all summers past. He began to dance — a jig of jubilance. Then as quickly as it had come this smell rolled away. The sun cleared the roofs of the houses and pierced the still sparse leafage of the trees. The air retreated to the austere distance of spring. At the end of the street, the screen of foliage darkened as though grown wet, then parted.

Out from the depths of the leaves came three young men. They strode abreast of one another, their shoulders jostling affectionately as though eager for the chafing of flesh against flesh. They laughed and now and then threw their heads back, and tousled one another's hair. They staggered slightly and fell against each other as they walked. The fabric of their t-shirts clung to their bodies in glimmering sheaths of sweat. The youth to the right held a ball cradled against his hip. But almost every second, the group dissolved into a struggling of legs and arms as the ball bounced about among them. Then once more they would walk abreast, laughing and drunk from their exertion, their sweat like an oil to ease the chafing of their broad shoulders. Always and unthinkingly the threesome regrouped with the same youth in the middle.

When one's cruel and secret craving for the flesh is found embodied in a being who is the craving of one's heart, that desire, no matter how unnameable, how inconceivable, how unmentionable to another, must at least be admitted to oneself. At the sight of this man, this boy, this youth who strode in the middle surrounded by the love of his comrades, Lear was hollowed as by the sighting of a god — a god manifest in the vulnerable flesh, hollowing Lear's heart as this man's beauty hollowed the air through which he walked, hollowing Lear's heart to hold the truth of his desire — a truth so long held hushed within him, not daring to be thought, that the simple fact of uttering it to himself in this one silent flash made his entrails weep.

He desired this man in the flesh — openly, flagrantly, if only to himself. And the sudden coupling of this desire with love gave him the glorious and terrifying sensation of strength to fulfill his desire.

His eyes were serpentine tongues that lashed round his love's body — tongues of passion that writhed over him more rapidly than flames, existing on every part of him at once. One tongue crept shuddering round his neck to delve into the hollows of his ears, to drink from his eyes and fan at the flower of his nostrils. Before they had come three steps closer to one another, Lear had robbed him of his clothes and they rolled together on the lawn, their lips attacking one another in a frenzy of hunger so akin to drowning they were forced to claw up chunks of black dirt and stuff it into their mouths to save themselves.

They drew closer and Lear smelled the flower of his love's sweat, as clearly demarcated from the sweat of his comrades as the timbre of his laughter. And then the realization of the horror of his desire swept over him and he dropped his eyes.

Beyond this fatal point of drawing closer, he knew he could no longer look at his love. Not until his love had passed him by and was already on the road to being gone from him — away, irretrievably away. For if their eyes met, his love would see in Lear's eyes what had been done to him, this secret rape. And his eyes would wall themselves high with anger and revulsion. And his love and the friends of his love would beat him into the ground so deep the soles of his love's feet crashing on his lips would not impregnate them with a lone weed.

He passed them in a stony daze and felt the hot wind from their bodies push him aside.

When they were gone from him for half a minute he turned round once to know his love from behind. And in that one brief view he knew he would recognize that back anywhere, at any distance — his love like an anatomy lesson held before him — the unreachable, untouchable anatomy not made for his desire.

He did not know if his love had looked at him. And if he had, what would he have seen? He would have seen an old man who hid a child — the child visible perhaps in Lear's wrists, his throat, his fingers — as though the child clung to him there, or he to it — but in the eyes an old toothless hunger looking wordlessly after the flesh, as one who, though grown old, had never learned love's language, having frightened it too much by the consciousness of something ugly but only half forgotten hidden beneath his beard.

He turned back toward the screen of foliage. But when he got there he saw it did not mask the wilderness. It was only a thin screen, a curtain row of early leafing trees with high, white trunks as thin and supple as shoots. Beyond them lay a diamond-shaped park, thinly wooded so that its perfect geometry could be seen at a glance. All round this park tree-lined streets led off into the distance like the spokes of a giant wheel. And farther out, seemingly beyond the curve of the earth, turrets of factories and gleaming, glass-clad high-rises pierced the thin air.

A hunger for older, more decayed, less wholesome neighborhoods took hold of him. And he struck back toward the heart of the city, but by a different street.

XI

The trees have grown younger
and the stones of the wall gone back to a time
when they were to us older than mankind.

XII

The wall had always been there, by the edge of the park. But somehow it had escaped his notice. It was a high brick wall covered with patches of moss and crumbling stucco. He followed the wall in its slow meanderings, irrational as though its curves followed the dictate of a stream hidden on its other side. When he reached the gate he stepped through so impulsively he didn't notice until it was too late the guard stationed in the little wooden booth. His first instinct was to turn back. He stopped for an instant in panic. But as the guard simply watched him, he continued to advance — ashamed somehow at the thought of turning and retreating under the gaze of this stranger.

As he passed the guard he concentrated on the sign propped beside his booth:

BOTANICAL GARDENS

Open 7 days a week

9AM til dusk

Entry Free

He had done it. He was inside. And he had entered without even thinking. Had he known about the guard, it might have taken weeks to find the courage to walk in front of him. He was in the botanical gardens!

He fell in love with the place immediately and decided that this was where he would like to live. He had never felt so safe as in this place where trees had sanctuary.

He felt that he had entered another world, but could not describe to himself in what the difference lay. In some parts of the garden he was in a different time altogether — a time where love trysts and bitter betrayals, murder, the waste of youthful beauty, the unhoped-for answering of inexpressible desires — all these human passions had been played according to the rules of another age beneath the hushed massings of trees that must have been old even then and wise enough to keep those secrets they witnessed — a girl emboldened by desire slipping between the trunks of two oaks, planning a desperate escape, searching with her ears to unravel the quiet breathing of her horse from the distant music of the ball — a servant moving across the night lawn toward a deadly exchange of notes, the vellum in his hand poisoned with sweet words — a glass of laughter shattered by a throat so impulsive as to betray itself to an ear ill met in the shadows — blood, a little flower that blooms once and grows downward without roots.

In other parts of the garden it was not time that changed so much as place. Amidst the exotic flowering of unknown trees he was transported to some orient that had not betrayed its antiquity, where beneath the weight of 5,000 years of recorded death, a young prince spied on the court ladies' nudity with the guiltlessness of Murasaki.

In this garden of paths laid out so as not to disturb the trees, he felt conversely to their power his own humanity flourish within him. And he sat flagrantly on a bench beside a beech-lined walk, as though it were his right to do so. He sat there for some time thinking of love, imagining countless stories, intrigues in which he played a speaking part. His lips emboldened by an echoing ear unlocked years of unvoiced fancies. And whose was this echoing ear? Once the man is found it is impossible to recapture that imagining of him when he has not yet been seen. He was perhaps a hand, a thigh, a throat, all rife with the portent of a sex, rather than the face whose individual beauty would have been unimaginable.

As he mused, it did not occur to him to think that passionate love was his main ambition in life. Yet in the end it was. But this urgent, overwhelming desire was strangely coupled with a longing towards the inhuman. Only in that vacant, unapproachable zone, his sorrow could fulfill itself.

In his isolation he was exceedingly powerful — subject to no restraint of self-consciousness except that ultimate restraint of remaining completely hidden — subject to no one's thought except his own — although never having had to voice his thoughts, it would be hard to say whether he truly thought at all. At times he did think, often perhaps, through the language of books. But mainly he was a creature of perception, thriving on his ecstatic senses. When he read he entered into books as this same creature. Inside each book, inside that forested snail shell, that jewel box of lives constantly replaying themselves according to the laws of ultimate death, he wandered as the ecstatic creature he was — looking out the window at the barren branches of the trees while behind him in the drawing room the countess wrote her desperate love note. And on the next page, while the man to whom her secret note was addressed strangled the beautiful laundress, he smelled for her, as she died, the odors of decaying leaves into which she would fall.

So charged was his potential love with the weight of drama and of death, with ultimate longing for sorrow, that a creature whom he might have loved and who could bear to hear the declaration of his love (if he dared declare its true nature) without recoiling in horror, would have been a rare creature, almost inconceivable.

But in the power of his isolation he believed in such a being, as though through the power of his belief he could make this creature exist — not a god but a fleshly being he would force into life — a fleshly god not separated from him by any childhood but full-sprung at birth into the vigor of manhood, as are certain antique gods.

He rose and walked.

When first he saw the house through the trees, he thought it was a body of water. This illusion lasted for some seconds — the high windowless wall completely filling all the gaps between the branches as though the trees stood at its edge and it were the pale surface of a lake stacked before his vision. Then he saw the cornicing and the green copper of the roof. The pathway turned. Before him a brick walk led up to a raised terrace that supported the steps of the portico.

The house was beautiful, built in a neo-classic style made almost tomblike by the stern and heavy proportions of its elements. Thick moldings shrouded high windows, the windows spaced widely apart so that the house seemed shadowed from without, a house of thick walls containing. The columns of the portico were so fat that at a distance he wondered if he would be able to squeeze between them. Each step that led down from the porch flaunted its tonnage. Yet the steps flanked the porch in graceful semi-curves that somehow deviated from themselves, as though this simple curve were a function of spiraling out of itself.

Above the portico a copper dome adorned the central axis of the house. This green hemisphere seemed biblically heavy as it rested on its square stuccoed base. He sensed the stucco of the walls masked bricks, laid to create the effect of massive stonework.

This megalithic pre-Victoriana striving for classical grace was a masterpiece of time's density — time clasped within these walls so hungrily that on the day it was completed this house must have seemed archaic, dating from some past that never existed, beckoning its inhabitants toward that past.

As he approached he saw at the top of the steps hung between the columns a velvet rope with a sign that read:

NOT OPEN TO THE PUBLIC
STAFF ONLY

Slowly he mounted the deep stone steps, feeling with his body the curve their wide spiral imposed on his approach. He stopped at the rope and peered across the portico at the doorway. It was flanked by square pilasters that supported a massive jutting lintel. The double doors were open onto the shadow of the house. He could see nothing of the interior. A few feet beyond the door a parquet floor dangled over the lip of shadow.

"STAFF"... He tried to conjure what that word might imply in relation to this house, this garden. He thought of some 19th-century psychiatric sanitarium. Perhaps Freud had been cloistered in the library of this house for most of the past century, writing discursive letters, absentminded of the fact that they were never sent, that he never broke his concentration long enough to look for a reply, or die. Somehow this house escaped an institutional air. He was certain that it had not lost its original nature and that at least part of it was truly inhabited.

He tried to walk round the exterior of the house but realized he could not. The house intersected the high brick wall that surrounded the gardens. This then was a house that gave onto two worlds — on one side the garden, on the other the street.

A large complex of greenhouses abutted one wing of the house. Their wrought iron superstructure looked Victorian in its intricacy, of a later date than the main house. Behind thick leaden panes of glass a maze of vines and branches rose purple and grey. The sun had grown dusty and fat with the lengthening of afternoon. A droning luminescence clung to the glass walls and reverberated in a yellow haze. The jungle behind the glass was slowly converging toward a silhouette.

He saw no doorway, no possible opening in the glass through which this jungle might be entered. A field of gigantic fleshy flowers separated the walkway from the greenhouse. These flowers were planted in strict linear pattern, and rose up on thick stalks to the level of his face. Every flower was trained out toward the walk.

As he looked at them they seemed so many faces staring back at him. Each fleshy hollow was a face, an open mouth that contained a sex rather than an eye, a seeing sex. All round this sex the face, which was the gaping hollow of a mouth, emitted a deep, slow scream of warning, warding him off. This scream varied in depth and intensity with the color of each flower. But every color was a scream of warning in the burning afternoon. Beyond the guardian flowers a high hedge of boxwood masked the lower walls of the greenhouse.

He advanced onto the exposed earth from which these flowers sprang. The earth was deeply tilled and soft. His feet sank into it. But just before they vanished they reached a firmer level that supported him. As he passed through each rank of flowers, they did not turn round to him. He continued to advance.

It would be hard to say what imperious desire compelled him to force his way through the tangle of the boxwood — almost as an insect burrows its way through a thick barrier of flesh toward the rich blood within. This intricate screen of leafage was not so impassible as it looked. All the leaves had been trained out to create an opaque screen. But behind their dense tangling the hedge was a long hollow — a hall of jagged branches through whose interlockings he managed to twist with ease.

He remained slightly within the zone of branches, suspended from them as from a web. From within this shadowed hollow he could see with great clarity the interior of the greenhouse.

The light trapped within this huge shell of glass was liquid and green. There everything happened with undulating slowness. Perhaps nothing happened other than the snaking of the vines, so massive as to become confused with the trees through which they twisted. But in this purple canopy something seemed to happen with a slowness that was perhaps only the verge of an event, or was even the opposite of slowness — the insane rapidity of something ordinarily so slow as to be unseeable, here verging on sight.

A man appeared from round a curve in one of the walkways. He moved deliberately, looking about at the overhanging canopy of vines. He wore a suit so dark as to be an invisibility. It erased his flesh. All that could be seen of him were his head and hands. He carried a knife. The first impression Lear got of him was of a great solitude. This solitude frightened Lear — so that he could not bear to look at the man' s face, could not bear to see this solitude so such more massive, truer, more potent than his own. But he watched the man's hands, hypnotized.

The hand that did not hold the knife seized a fat vine that hung across the path. The hand caressed the vine, squeezing it. The vine began to undulate like an immensely thick yet supple rope. The hand interrupted, alternated the rhythm of the vine's undulations so that they became incredibly lifelike, serpentine, self-generated. Then slowly, gently, the hand moved along the vine, questing to untangle the stem of a particular leaf, heavier, broader than its fellows. The knife-bearing hand reached up and with a quick motion severed the leaf at the point where it sprang from the vine's thick shaft. The man placed the leaf in the breast pocket of his jacket. The leaf disappeared beneath that cloak of invisibility. At the same time he drew out from somewhere in that breast a glass vial. The knife disappeared somewhere about the region of the man's hip. One hand now held the vial beneath the gash in the vine while the other hand, curled round it, squeezed.

The wound in the vine was incredibly white. It ached in the pallor of its exposure. From this wound a crystalline strand dangled, lengthening slowly, elastically toward the mouth of the vial. Lear began to shudder. He felt this wound on his own flesh. He felt the languorous draining of blood from his eyes, his chest. He exhaled his very being, prey to the manipulation of those hands — skillful, purposeful, ultimately erotic, ultimately detached. He felt those hands at work on his own flesh, and welcomed the wound they had inflicted.

He looked back at the man's face. Now, rather than desiring to avert his gaze, he did not want to take his eyes away from it — except at times to travel back to those pale hands that continued to bleed the vine. From the hands to the face, from the face to the hands — what unknown, perhaps eternally hidden territory he traversed in that journey. The hands were expressive of a strange combination of qualities — refined, graceful. Yet the overall structure of the hand revealed an extreme masculine solidity, expressive of great physical prowess. The head, poised on a throat of columnar strength, likewise was powerful and refined. Nothing could be more revealing, more painfully elegant, than the angle at which the bridge of that nose arched away from the brow, nothing more enchanting than the slight curve of that upper lip, which belied the stern mouth beneath, almost grim in its repose. The eyes, gazing up at the vine, curved away from one another almost sorrowfully. This head, in its strength and its solemnity, the curve of that brow, those dark eyes containing the curve of the earth — became for Lear a temple — a temple made from a material more potent than rock, designed according to a magic harmony of chance — centuries of genetic happenstance conjoining for one brief life in a perfect imperfection, virile, harmonious, human, unimaginable. How could he have mistrusted this face, desired to look away from it?

Lear would learn that this man whose motions were so studied, so solemn, could at times in the course of his work move with an almost clinical rapidity. These intervals were so surprising that, although happening directly before his eyes, at times they went unseen so that the man seemed to displace himself magically.

Before Lear had time to realize what had happened, those hands had closed and pocketed the vial and tied an almost ludicrous bandage about the wounded vine. And when Lear's eyes shifted to marvel at these whirring hands, the man turned away so that Lear did not have time to get a last glimpse of his face. He was quickly swallowed by the jungle.

Lear was bereft. Never had he felt such desolation. Suddenly the jungle terrified him. He felt it staring out at him. He squirmed to disentangle himself from the hedge, to remove his face from the cold glass against which the face of the jungle was pressed towards him.

The walkway had been swallowed by shadow. In the distance he saw a dragnet of guards moving in a sweep of the park. Hurriedly he looked for an exit, hoping to get out before being asked to leave.

XIII

In the park Lear found a small spade, which he kept and carried with him at all times. It had a heavy wooden handle, darkened and smoothed through use. The iron digging bowl came to a sharp point, like an animal's tooth, capable of penetrating the hardest earth. Sometimes at the edge of the stagnant and forgotten lake where he bathed, he would dig holes. At times these holes would quickly ooze up with water, drowning up to the level of the lake. But in certain spots he could keep the holes dry for long periods — slowly hollowing away the isthmus of land that separated the hole from the lake until finally this shell wall crumbled and the hole was consumed by the waters. During rainstorms he rarely disturbed existent puddles but at times created puddles of his own, channeling their forms from one to another through the softened earth. A puddle at the foot of a tree would cause the tree to vault shackled to itself in the sky. Sometimes he came upon strange networks of tuberous white roots whose exposure shocked and hypnotized, smooth dense rocks that tore away from their deep sockets of clay with such a protesting suckage that he reburied them, in spite of their beauty. In the cemetery fragments of wrought iron, old hinges, anything he unearthed held a special fascination. But he was afraid to disturb anything he found there and always solemnly reburied it.

XIV

When he waited beside the greenhouse Lear imagined himself to be a statue. This was not a picturing of himself from without, but a stoniness that spread outward from his chest and a cold yet thrilling languor that held him. This languor was sorrowful — almost a mourning of one's own death. Its source was unfindable. From somewhere at his center it sounded as from the secret chamber of a conch shell, then broke over him in a curve that shadowed him and clasped his skin in a cold cloak. At these times his vision had no focus. Yet he perceived with great clarity — not objects so much as their existence. The trees were less corporeal objects than things that existed in motion — constantly retreating, drawing back on the verge of a hush in which their perspective would turn itself inside out, reveal them as trees on the edge of another, advancing world in which light had the power of water — to drown, to uproot, to tear away, but also to uphold. In this strange deep, smells were creatures. Smells were the voice of things.

As a statue, waiting was a pleasure to him, and was not so much waiting as another form of existence. In this state he could watch the man through the glass as though he were a ghost watching him. It did not occur to him to think it strange, his watching of this man. He held as much communion with him as a ghost could, silent of necessity, and distanced. He called this man The Man Who Loves Plants.

Anyone else who watched with such devotion would have learned much more about this man and his habits than Lear did. They might have learned at what times of day he was most likely to enter the greenhouse. They might have gained some inkling of the type of research in which he was engaged. But Lear learned none of these things. He did not spy on this man, he simply watched him. And for him this watching was a great intimacy in which no questions need be asked. The science of this man's discipline did not concern him. He was fascinated, though, by the way in which this man looked at the trees. During his walks through the greenhouse he could stand lost in thought for unnameable stretches. Yet his thoughts, though silent and turned inwards, seemed to quest for some answer from his surroundings. As he walked, his eyes roved ponderously over the jungle around him, searching for something. At these times Lear longed to call out, to beat against the glass. But he could not bring himself to do so.

A ghost's intimacy with the flesh is cold and distant, a bone-fingered hunger clawing at the locks. This man always wore black suits, lab coats, tightly buttoned shirts — as though a strange erasure of the flesh had left him only head and hands, and a bit of his throat, to be revealed. And yet this very masking gave Lear a shuddering consciousness, a premonitory smell of all that mysterious territory traversed in his imagined roamings between the head and the hands, the hands and the feet. In his imaginings he explored this unknown territory as a ghost would, in a smokelike and all-enveloping sheath, snaking about his love, existing on every part of him simultaneously like a liquid glove. He imagined this flesh as pale and cold, yet pungent. He thought of it as food.

"Your shadow holds your magic, black like your thigh, but pale and cold when stripped."

He crouched beneath the boxwood and, as he thought this, picked away with his fingers at the leading that anchored the pane of glass before him. His fingers bled, and he saw with great joy the blood stain the glass. Perhaps if the rain did not wash it away, this stain would betray him. His blood would give this ghost a voice.

XV

He gazed in shock at what he had unearthed. Running his spade lightly through the loose white dirt — almost a mixture of fine sand and pebbles — at the base of a mausoleum, he had uncovered a package of disposable razors. He lifted the package. The loose earth fell away. The plastic wrapper was completely unopened. He laid the package back in the shallow hole and pressed his hand palm down atop it. The plastic was warm from the earth. With his right hand he quickly filled in the hole he had made. But he kept his left hand pressed against the package of razors so that this hand was also buried. The earth was warm on his hand where it lay buried in a patch of sunlight.

The day was idyllic, with a silent power that can only be attained by a day in a cemetery. All round him the air stirred, coaxing perfumes from the earth, the grass. The trees moved with the sound of waves, and the passage of birds was as silent as the passage of the shadows of small clouds. To watch the small grains of sand stir in the sunlight to the slight quivering of his buried hand was hypnotic. He had never felt so peaceful. He had never felt such horror. He could not bring himself to pull those razors out from the earth. Yet there was no way he could withdraw his hand and leave them buried. He was rooted to the ground, his buried hand rooting him to those instruments of revelation.

What those razors might reveal filled him with fear. But more than this, his very fear of what they might reveal filled him with horror and shame at himself.

After a while he heard what could only be the sound of urination. Startled from his paralysis he looked up and saw through the bushes only a few feet away a man's penis spraying the earth. It jutted from a pair of dark trousers. After the ray of urine that shot from it had slowed to a dribble, the hand that held this penis began to caress it, squeezing and stretching it almost brutally, as though trying to force it beyond its limits of elasticity. Another man stepped silently up to the screen of bushes alongside the first. Lear could not see what he was doing, but he heard again the sound of urination. The two men continued to stand side by side long after this sound had stopped. A golden neck of urine snaked across the dirt toward his buried hand. But the dry earth swallowed this liquid snake before it reached him. He could not see the eyes of either man. They both wore hats and their eyes were masked. But he saw their mouths and chins, strangely similar to one another, strangely expressionless. The first man's penis was now rigid. It was extremely beautiful and throbbed in the cage of his fingers. Suddenly both men turned and disappeared around the side of the mausoleum against which Lear crouched. He heard them enter the vault, their sand-covered shoes grind against its stone floor. Apart from this, there was no other sound.

Lear did not feel any human emotion. At that instant every thought he had ever thought or failed to think, without even needing to be thought, attained a painful state of solidity inside his head — thoughts as solid and pointed as the spikes of the wrought iron fence that surrounded the cemetery, as sharp and bristling as the branches of all the pine trees across the face of the earth, as blinding as a noonday sun flashing across a field of broken glass. This whole world of things, as vast and myriad as the exterior world, but more real, more sharply edged, of a crueller, more self-conscious nature, grew inside his head — each thing a thought growing with the painful thought of its existence so that he felt the surface of his brain clawed and seared, it would be hard to say whether from within or from without. His buried hand had clenched the razors with such ferocity that it had shaken away the earth and lay exposed — a gnarled and frightening thing. He looked at it.

Suddenly his hand clasped the razors against his chest so violently that he bruised his breastbone. But he barely felt the pain. He ran from the cemetery with the razors in one hand and his spade in the other. He knew what he must do and that he must do it quickly.

He returned to the lake and, using its surface as a mirror, began hacking away at his beard with the disposable razors. One by one their edges were blunted by the severe task of cutting away his full growth of beard. He realized that he was using the razors more as scissors and that he would have to be careful not to exhaust them all on one side of his face — otherwise he would wind up a creature so shocking to look at, so laughable, that he would never be able to steal more razors. Yet he was in a complete frenzy — grim beyond thought, in an ultimate state of suspense — while at the same time exulting in advance at the hideousness he would uncover. He rotated from one razor to another, hacking away at his face until his skin was completely raw. He bled in patches. The blood seemed to ease the razor's passage over his skin, acting as an ointment.

His face emerged from the shadows. It was still obscured by thick stubble, a coarse, springy haze that veiled the raw flesh. And yet, gazing at the shadowy surface of the lake, he thought he could discern the true outline of his face. Shuddering, he dropped the last blunted razor, realizing he could accomplish no more with it. Wetting his hands, he ran them over his cheeks and jaw, bearing down in an attempt to crush the stubble flat, to feel out with his fingers whether this face that he discerned through the double haze of lake and beard were true.

The expected hideousness, the vacancy of the jaw, the wounded mouth, had not appeared. Certainly he looked rather mad, staring at himself so feverishly. But this madness, the threat of his eyes, appealed to him. The tragic destiny he had known to be written across his face as something painful to the eye had not been exposed. Not yet. But how could he be sure? The lake was not a true mirror, and his face was still obscured by thick stubble. He must rip off this veil entirely, expose his true face. He could not wait to see the truth. How had he waited so long? The suspense was maddening. He must steal more razors.

As he left the boundary of the park he expected passersby on the sidewalk to start back in shock and horror. But their lack of horror was no reassurance. None of these people knew him. Why should it matter to them how loathsome he was? He realized, now that he almost longed for them to look at him, that these people did not notice him. "You'd have to be truly deformed," he thought, "to get any reaction out of these people."

As he walked a billboard caught his eye and he stopped dead in his tracks. Shaving cream! Of course! How could he not have thought of it? But why should he have? Were he not a walking wound, he would have laughed at himself. Where did one get it?

He went into a large grocery store and wandered through the aisles for what seemed painful hours until he recognized the can from the billboard. As he reached for it he pictured himself doing so and saw himself as an emaciated and pitiful wretch compared to the giant in the billboard, pictured from his upper lip down to some point on his broad chest just above his nipples — his cleft chin and chiseled lips half obscured by shaving cream.

The razors were hung right in front of the cash registers, which presented some difficulty. But he had never been driven by such overwhelming determination, not even when prey to the most agonizing hunger. He did not have a cent. He grabbed the razors and ran from the store, not bothering to conceal his thievery. He ran for blocks, but could not tell if anyone had attempted to follow him. He returned to the park. As he approached it he felt that he approached the moment when he would commit an irreversible act, akin to suicide.

This second shaving was more terrible than the first. His exultation in his own loathsomeness was gone. The thin veil of beard that remained had perhaps given him a false hope of redemption. And now he must tear this veil away again. How many times would he have to tear it away? He almost could not bear to look at himself as he shaved. As each swath of shaving cream fell from his face it landed in the waters and obscured his reflection. Sometimes he did not wait for the ripples to subside before he cut another swath. When he did look down he implored his face — a thousand prayers contained in each immeasurable instant, so that each instant strained under the agony of containing his imploring. A century passed in the accomplishment of this simple act which held for him the import of his own death. The final stroke of the razor took place in the water. He was captive of his reflection. He stared at himself until the light failed. Then he left the park in search of other mirrors.

In the dusk beside the park a girl waited by the bus stop. He lingered among the trees a moment to watch her. The streetlamp beneath which she stood had captured and retained the lurid sunset, already long gone down the street that seemed to reach the earth's curve. The streetlamp held this light already dead in a cone above her. Looking down the street toward there from where the bus would come, she was extremely still. This lent her an air of sorrow, and Lear felt the shuddering of the inanimate as he looked at her. Her clothing seemed to him antiquated and severe. Yet her face, the eyes converging toward the distance, was extremely beautiful. The bus approached with a low-pitched drone that reminded him of the passage of distant trucks on wet highways. She boarded it. The bus moved on into the night, rocking slightly, windows alight. Behind him the park exhaled a wet, cold smell. The streetlamp for a second caught the billowing of trees' night. Looking after the bus he imagined it traveling toward isolated destinations, outskirts, slums, city limits. He mourned his life unlived.

That night he looked in many mirrors. Each one he approached with shuddering expectation — as though at the fatal moment when he stepped before it, leapt into it, this new mirror might belie the revelation that had been given him, unveil the true monstrosity that up till now had been hidden by the play of the light — streetlamps, flashing signs, the headlights of passing cars. He took mirrors as he found them. The city was for him that night a hall of mirrors in which he wished to lose himself ever more deeply — windows of houses, windows of cars and stores, some rare mirror in a shopfront on an isolated street where he could linger to gaze at himself, not forced to pretend beneath the eyes of passersby that his life did not depend on what he saw. At some point he found himself in the recessed entrance to a Woolworth's, surrounded by mirrored columns. The perspective of the columns allowed him to see himself from many angles, so that he stood in a hall of himself and around him the street dwindled away in all directions. Few people were abroad at this hour. He grew oblivious to them.

As he looked at himself, he mourned his life unlived. Yet he felt that he had been granted another life, monstrous perhaps, yet not crippled, not unappealing to his eye. His face possessed an animal harmony akin to the haughty skulls of certain wild things — some creature half deer, half bird of prey. He fell in love with himself and with the power he possessed — both a power of action and a power to be loved.

The night was filled with expectation and yet expected nothing but itself. He wandered through the night. The night was filled with power. Sheet lightning bristled in the treetops. Along dark residential streets the flowers in the front yards moved on a hot wind flowing from a region of approaching rain. He leapt and danced, feeling himself a child, wild with expectation, yet mourning his unlived life, on the verge of laughter, pitying all who slept.

When the rain began — a hot, steady rain before dawn — he sat in a field of weeds beside a railroad track. Weeping and yet wild with hunger, he made himself a mudpie from the blackest of earth. He ate it, imagining it to be chocolate cake.

XVI

The rain coursed down the walls of the greenhouse, plummeting in sheets along its walls. The greenhouse appeared to be a huge glass submarine surfacing out of the deep. The sky was dark as night. It rolled and sped. Beneath the canopy of boxwood he could barely see what he was doing as he chiseled away at the leading of the glass with the point of his spade. The rain gave him courage. Surrounded by the rain, his each action was cloaked in invisibility so that he could barely perceive his own hands hacking away, gnawing at the anchoring of the glass. The thunder drove him. The thunder was the audible approbation of what he did. Yet what he did was in no way an attempt to find shelter from the rain.

When the pane of glass gave, he managed to slide it away intact. The opening before him was like the lip of a giant bottle. It droned and emitted a strange suction. Before entering the greenhouse he removed his shoes and buried them in the mud beneath the boxwood. Though he would have thought trees should be naked, an unconquerable shame kept him from removing his clothes.

XVII

Love was horror. Though in later years he would look back on himself with a great tenderness, almost a jealous love for this boy who had been himself, this boy who had loved so much — jealous for that time, for the power of his love, the all-consuming nature of his suffering — as though now that the boy was gone from him, he could love him like another being, love his power to love and suffer, while strangely, his memory of the man this boy had loved was somewhat faded.

But at the time this man's existence was so powerful as to torture the daylight, streets seen out the window, objects he had touched — as though all things, living and inanimate, must suffer at every moment, as Lear did, the terrible fate of not being a part of this man he so loved.

Love was horror. The daylight was sharpened by it so that everything he saw was a blade to his eyes. Stabbed by everything, he was forced to move slowly through an air rife with blades so as not to gore himself through an inadvertent breath or gesture. He walked becalmed by horror.

Through years of solitary sorrowing he had grown so used to conceiving of his life as barren of events that he had long ago abandoned any ambition for a happiness outside of sorrow. But this horror that was love attacked the very foundation of his sorrow, for it sprang from a desire rooted not in solitude but in another human life. Because this love attacked and undermined his sorrow, it was a thing of horror. It left him with nothing. It was, above all, self-horror.

And yet this horror was as ecstatic as sorrow. More so. Of its very nature it was ecstatic. Wounded by sight and breath, he was torn from his flesh, disemboweled at every moment, his throat hatched out of itself. It was as though his sorrow had found an object. Love, by its very hopelessness, was glorified. Desire, by its monstrosity, became for him the perfect expression of the sorrowful nature of all things. He embraced this horror with all his heart.

Perhaps he might have been driven to reveal himself to The Man Who Loved Plants. But something about being hidden tends towards monstrosity. He had already gone too long unseen.

With his wild animal's sensibility he was driven to hide in the confines of that house as much as if he still wandered through any streets or parks. And as a wild animal hiding in that house would fail to perceive logically the structure of the rooms through which he wandered, this house was to Lear a vast, dark, and limitless domain of rooms and passageways that never repeated themselves according to any pattern that could be known. The house appeared to Lear's eyes as a limitless wooden hive branching out, radiating round the spiral of the staircase as around the vortex of a conch shell that encloses more and more chambers as it twists inward. During the day the walls seemed composed of such a chill thickness of masonry that, sheltered by those walls in some inner room with no windows, it would be possible to hide not only from the day but from the passage of time itself.

No one came into this wing of the house but the man Lear called his love, the botanist, Phillip Moravia. This man was solitary. Lear gloried in this man's solitary nature. And one thing he did notice, quickly and instinctively, was that the doors leading from this wing to parts of the house frequented during the day by other members of the garden's staff were always locked.

Entombed in this vastness of brick and stone alone with the one man he so dreaded and desired, Lear wandered through the hallways during the long days, hiding from Phillip Moravia, hiding even from the furniture. His mind was consumed with horrific visions of lust —

the sexual union between Phillip Moravia and himself always taking place on some dark stretch of earth wet with the night and so without confines in its darkness as to be a gullet or a grave. Each gesture of desire was coupled in his mind with murderous or suicidal intent, as though his desire could only be freed from the constraints of horror and of shame through death.

He raved with desire as he roamed through the hallways of that house. But he gloried in his solitary ravings like a megalomaniac — the bitter truth of desire's monstrosity seeping through his skin to sear anything he touched. The furniture, stained by the acid of his desire, stared back at him with forbidding judgement. Most of the furniture in that house was so old and untouched by the uses of humanity that, high, dark and severe with age, it seemed to date from an epoch when people did not copulate. Lear cringed before the furniture, at times protesting, thinking — But people must have lusted under these tables, on these beds, otherwise how would we all be here?

At times, embracing his horror with all his heart, he gloried in his most abject gestures. He could not make a single gesture that was not the product of his obsession. He was driven to his every action — tight-lipped, his chilled and pallid face on the verge of raining sweats, almost against his will.

Every day at some dead hour of the afternoon when he knew or sensed that Phillip Moravia was gone from that wing of the house and would not be able to surprise him, a kind of hypnosis would take hold of him in which, calm but filled with dread, he was drawn toward Phillip Moravia's room. He never actually tried to resist the lure of that room. Yet every step he took towards it, every gesture he made inside it, filled him with such a sense of criminality that it felt as though he had tried to resist entering that room but failed.

Inside that room he first closed all the windows. The sun protested and seemed as though it were trying forcibly to crawl in through the old glass of the windows during that stretch of days when, obstinately, it refused to rain and the summer had aged, shrivelled by illumination. But the air trapped inside the room thickened, blued, turned cool in a matter of instants, and all round him the objects in the room grew buoyant, floated off on a dark current. He stood in the middle of this room filled with secrets, his vision unfocussed, hazed, but shockingly sensitive, while all round him sacred objects bobbed and revolved majestically on some slow, merry-go-round current of the deep. Whether he looked at it or not, the door leading to the hall, which he had closed delicately, secretly behind him, was present to his vision as though it were a door in the back of his skull. And at every instant he thought he heard harsh, accusatory footsteps racing down the corridor, pounding louder and louder as they drew closer to that door about to be flung open onto his shame. But inside that room an ineffable calm reigned, the calm of the deep.

He would have liked to stay in that room for hours, watch the light fail. For here at the very source of his sorrow he was lulled into a sort of catalepsy in which his flesh might have become stone, his chambered heart as still as the interior of the armoire or the pigeon holes hidden by the heavy top of the writing desk. But beyond a certain length of time, fear got the better of him. The danger of discovery grew too great and he was forced to leave. Yet the time spent in that room was so surcharged with desire as to be stretched out of all conceivable measure. The only measure he could give it was the threat of those footsteps, always racing towards the door but never reaching it, always impending.

The air trapped within the room began to curdle about the mouldings of the windows. Large, slow blossoms of odor uncurled from the walls, took flesh from the thickened air, and hung on it. In the unnatural stillness, smells unfurled from the bed clothes, from crevices in the settling of the heavy furniture, from the woodwork. His nostrils were trained ecstatically toward the odor of Phillip Moravia's flesh, invisible sheaths of it, translucent grey sloughings of skin and sweat, dangled from the bedposts and wafted in tatters all round him. Shredded webs of flesh tugged and undulated before the mirror. His each slow inhalation was a consuming of Phillip Moravia's flesh, his secret smell. For Lear, these odors were the most intimate knowledge of Phillip Moravia he could steal.

In the stillness of that room his shame achieved such an intense communion with the humbleness of those lifeless objects around him, lying as though abandoned, that his shame was aggrandized, ennobled, became a state of mourning.

Sometimes, consumed by this state, he didn't move or touch anything for a long time. Sometimes he would crouch in a corner between the back of an upholstered armchair and the bookcase. Squatting there, pressing his cheek against the back of the chair as against the trunk of a giant sleeping woman, he would abandon himself to the smells that collected in this forgotten corner — smells of dust, the wood of the floor exhaling hollows like empty nut shells, the smell of cracks in the walls and of stories cooked out of the bindings of old books by the passage of the sun.

Sometimes he would lie down on the floor and stare into the darkness beneath the bed. His hand, with the impulse of a large spider, crawled under the bed on the stem of his arm, exploring. Sometimes he would pull out a shoe. Holding it so that it loomed close up to his face and it seemed in the shadows that he might crawl into it, he mused over the manliness of its architecture. Sometimes he placed his sex inside the shoe and, thrusting, felt it strain against the recesses that had held Phillip Moravia's toes. After a while he would withdraw from the shoe and study again its mysterious and manly architecture. His sense of horror was so acute that he was too hollowed to carry out the motions of desire. Quickly he would cover his sex, not daring to look at it.

He dared touch very few things in that room. A supreme chastity of gesture was imposed on him by his self-horror. If he drew open a drawer of the tall chest beside the mirror, he did not dare let his hand delve into it, only running his hand as lightly as possible across the skin of its contents. His hand shuddered all the while with the desperation of one who must restrain himself from shaking a corpse in a brute attempt to force life back into it.

If a piece of clothing had been left strewn somewhere in a state of such disarray that it would not be possible to tell he had disturbed it, then and only then he would lift it carefully with both his hands and bury his face in it. Hidden in the darkness of the cloth as in a nighttime of odors, he would sniff out traces of the sweet flesh it had contained. Or if the covers of the bed had been left flung back, exposing the crumpled sheets, then and only then he would climb onto the bed and run his forehead, his nose, his face across the sheets in languorous arcs, turning his head from side to side all the while like someone begging, "No... No," over and over. Whenever he crouched like this, he felt a blade suspended above his neck. As he coaxed the perfume of his love's sweat from the sheets, he waited for the blade to fall, for his neck to be severed. When after a while, collecting himself, he sat up and reluctantly took back his life, he would look up at the corners of the ceiling — cruelly distant, letting him live, not concerning themselves with him. And outside he felt the day abandon him, rush over him — this day he could have wandered through but now ignored.

Then he would go into the bathroom and, taking up Phillip Moravia's razor, shave himself before the mirror. Something about the simple nature of this act brought home to him with a kind of bitter pride how unnatural such simple acts of life were to him. As he wielded the blade he knew he committed a robbery, a perverse theft of intimacy with its master. And he was filled with a defiance that was the vengeful abandonment of all hope.

In the bedroom he did not dare look at himself in the mirror. He knew his sickened soul to be so powerful with horror that one look at himself would burn his image there and leave it lingering for Phillip Moravia to see. But here he could look at himself. For some reason in the bathroom mirror he could look at himself. Here, rather than burn itself into the glass, his reflection fell away, lost substance. The only thing that kept his image afloat, stopped it from sinking rocklike beneath the glass, was his eyes. As he shaved he looked at his eyes with such wonderment for all the sorrow of life within them that, though mouthless, he half expected them to scream — some sweet, discordant cry of despair from his eyes. As he ran the blade across his face he waited with a kind of detached curiosity for it to slit his cheek — for a rich wedge of red blood to open up across his face — a curtain drawn back before a wounded landscape that would pour out of him.

The light of afternoon, falling aslant the deep recess of the bathroom window, was caught in the delicate cracks veining the tiles of the walls around him. The room held back for a moment in a net of porcelain the day's passage, which he ignored. Gazing at the translucent bone lip of the sink cupping the daylight, and at the light plummeting down the rope of water from the spigot, he felt the day abandon him, rush over him, this day he could have wandered through but now ignored.

Each gesture he made inside that room, made against his will, reminded him of a time when he would not have needed to make these gestures — as though his desire had transformed time, thickened and debased it, so that he was distanced from the ecstatic shock of every instant. As he reached out to touch the clothing Phillip Moravia had so unthinkingly sanctified with his flesh, clothing strewn about as though dirtied, not sanctified — a shirt, a pair of pants, some underwear as chastely ivoried with stains as the mottled plaster of an old wall — to lift these relics to his face, he felt as though he reached for something else as well, or failed to reach for it.

He didn't know what this thing was, but that it had existed in other rooms, in his childhood. And he reached for it as though reaching blindly through a wall that separated him from what he once had been.

He thought of the great dark rooms of his childhood in which he had mourned so freely, as though it were a necessity and a right to mourn, not knowing this mourning would one day be reduced to a desire for the flesh of others. He thought of the one small disused bedroom fitted in behind the curve of the upstairs banister, as though one must follow a catwalk to reach it. He moved towards that room, a child full of hideous secrets, in the afternoon when his Mother was downstairs and other children were out playing (though it would never have occurred to him to think of other children except with fear). Only the most secret and uncontrollable of desires would have driven him upstairs alone once dusk attacked the windows and chopped the top of the staircase from its moorings. But it was still the afternoon and, driven by the explosions of his heart, he moved towards that one small disused bedroom in which a giant bed was trapped — the bed on which his father had died before his birth.

The bed was high and massive. It seemed to have gotten caught in the branches that jutted up against the windows. Only such an act could have borne this great bed up into this little room that itself seemed to hang from the trees. The bed consumed the room. A narrow aisle ran along one side, and round its foot. But this aisle was buried with stacks of books piled up almost to the height of the mattress so that there was not one inch of floor to be seen. To enter the room he was forced to hoist himself up onto the bed. Pushing against the door, which opened inwards, he could barely shove back the morass of books far enough to make a crack to slip through. Reaching up, he would grab one of the wooden pineapples that adorned the bedstead and drag himself up onto it.

Then he was truly alone, almost entombed in light. For the two high windows at the bed's foot, facing one another on this corner of the house, seemed bigger, taller than the room itself. The only thing bigger than them was the bed, trapped between books, barren walls, and branches. Barricaded into this room by the weight of the books, by their depth, their ancience, by the inconceivability of how anything inside this room could have gotten there — then even the trees, the day outside the window became a tomb to him — tomb of the afternoon's steadfast light.

Across the narrow aisle of books was a chest of drawers and, atop it, a mirror. The drawers could not be opened. They were sealed shut by the masonry of books in which the room was buried. He could force open the top drawer just far enough to glimpse a crack of darkness, but nothing of what it contained. Nor could he tell what was hidden beneath the bed. But he knew there must be many things down there. In this house there was no closet that was not stacked with secrets, no bed beneath which objects had not been forgotten in darkness — all, it seemed, from a century before his birth.

He had excavated a narrow shaft through this earthen depth of books. Hanging on the edge of the bed, he could grope down to pull lost things up from the deep. But there was a point beyond which he dared not reach — as though his hand, scuttling down so far from sight, might pull him down with it or fall prey to a spider.

But he had already found the one thing he was destined to find in that room. It was a book that revealed to him what every child is destined to learn — the harrying and irreversible vigor of his own sex — and its purpose, its use — a thing which can be explained so simply, almost a matter of course, but the consciousness of which, once set in motion, never ceases to gnaw away at us. He might have learned about the sexual act in many different ways. His Mother would never have told him. But even in his isolation he was bound to have chanced upon some lewd magazine, some risqué novel, and puzzled it together. Instead he had found a huge volume entitled *The Basic Writings of Sigmund Freud.*

There was no telling why he had even bothered to open this book. But what he learned there was such a revelation that, had he tried, he would not have been able to remember what it was like to be that other boy who, innocently, had opened that book for the first time. A whole new world of horror and of awe had been revealed to him. His sex unfurled between his legs as he read, took on a life, a pulse that almost consumed his being. How he understood the Latin names for forbidden parts of the body it would be hard to say. But he understood them in a flash. The words lay on the page ancient and shocking as though printed there, hidden there by God.

He read the dreams of hysterical German housewives and impotent burgomeisters whose revulsions and suppressed desires had already been swallowed by the passage of a century. After each dream Freud laid forth his interpretation, branding "penis" a hat stand or a clock, some descending roadway flanked with shrubs a "mons veneris" or "vagina." The very act of reading the names of these secret zones of the body, hidden, hushed, forbidden to thought, of seeing them laid out boldly in the print of an old book, caused giant penises to dance through the darkness of his head, a vast sexual landscape to stretch out across the darkness that was the nighttime of his wakeful imaginings when, closing his eyes in the depths of those afternoons, of a sudden all was desire.

He shuddered and crouched. Perched high atop that huge bed that must once have known other, more wholesome pleasures, he looked in the mirror and could not see himself. He was too guilty to see himself. His sex was his only reflection. When first the white blood flowed from him he looked down at himself in horror and thought — *My God, I have wounded myself beyond repair.* Then, lured back to that room each afternoon, to that book, to the unearthing of his sex, he discovered that he could wound himself again and again.

The irreversible gift of desire had been given him by a gentleman writing scholarly treatises in another century. His fingers clawed the edges of the book like an ugly secret, ready to slam it shut and shove it under the covers at the sound of an approaching footstep. He treated that book with awe and shamed reverence, like the filthiest of pornography.

He eyed his sex longingly from his enforced distance. And he did not think of his father who had died on this bed before he was born, nor for what reason this bed, these books had been put away, almost bricked up into this little room abandoned, disused, never visited. All was desire for him — desire for the trees, for the mournful cries of birds, for rain, for distance. But this new desire was hideous and secret, and this was why his Mother had put it away into this little room, buried it beneath a stack of books. But having found it, he was drawn toward it inexorably, every day — the afternoon calling to him through the hallways of the house, drawing him toward that secret, the afternoon become a lure, an irresistible urge toward his sexual abandon.

At the center of that room, his sex was no different than some mysterious old box he might have found in an attic, or some reflection in a mud puddle, magic as though reflecting from another world in which he could fly, or a landscape of rain seen out the window, wet tin rooftops filling him with awe of the sky — or the love of death itself. His sex might have been some beautiful corpse he imagined for the pleasure of mourning over it, or the roots of a tree that thrilled him with a deathly fascination. There was really no difference. This unexpected unearthing of his sex confirmed the solitude of all things — some old gloomy destiny he had found in a box under a bed. It had waited for him since before his birth and he was destined to find it, innocent little boy that he was, while rummaging through some attic.

The hot flow of white blood spurted from him as though erupting from the past, from some time before his birth. And the sorrowful emptiness that followed this spillage, the room settling back into its old dustiness but stained now with secret blood, confirmed for him the solitary nature of all things. He was alone before his sex, doubly alone before this other life, this other mind that had suddenly quickened between his legs — a child so fragile, so subject to death wishes, living outside of time, that it hardly seemed possible he could be a channel for this ancient force of life that threads time together.

And yet how glorious it was! He did not know what he desired then, had not yet dared conceive of this sex as something he could desire in another. He desired his own sexual prowess.

Cast adrift on that bed, entombed in light, too maddened with desire to see himself in the mirror, not breaking the shell of dust that veiled it, he abandoned himself to this secret and horrifying act. Dark pockets of dust weighted down the swathings of the curtains as diaphanous as old curdled light before the windows. Dust shone in spun purple across the submerged wall of books that surrounded him. At any moment he might be discovered. The air itself watched him. The sky at the tops of the windows watched him. His Mother, or some old accusatory gnome taken flesh from the walls, might fling open the door and surprise him curled over his shame. Yet how glorious it was! And he could not have expected it to be different. He had not yet conceived of love then. But once having done so, how could he have expected any joy in love? Here in Phillip Moravia's room, all was still desire, still secret and horrifying.

He was never found in that room, nor in any other room where he crouched alone before his sex. His sex jutted flagrant on the air, but never to be flaunted before another, never to know the domineering glory of that flaunting, that exposure. Some face he could almost imagine — was it a woman's, was it a man's — it was almost the face of some other child he might have imagined, with the serious, all-knowing eyes of childhood, borne stern and solemn as when a child goes secret through the house — some chaste, imaginary sister it was who peered silently through the crack of that door and caught him in the act. But try as he might, he could not imagine either the awe of revulsion or the awe of desire in those eyes as, gazing innocently through the crack of that door, she surprised him at the flaunting of his sex. It jutted on the air of afternoons so golden and so pure they could only seem old then. Though they lost their age from year to year til now they seemed only a thing of the present. His sex wounded the air. But in those imagined eyes surprising it, he could see to his satisfaction neither fascination nor disgust. But as that antique head turned away and flattened itself back into the wall of shadows, he read in those eyes averted with the discretion of ghosts an almost pitying comprehension — the wisdom of some sister better versed in the sorrows of desire and individuality. And though he longed to call her back, to force from her in a tantrum of screaming some betrayal of the longed-for hunger or revulsion, she was gone — her head eclipsed by its discreet turning away, eclipsed into a hollow that vanished on a thread, a crack unraveled by a doorway's shutting on the air.

XVIII

The day was long in its stillness, the potency of its sun. He did not mind the length of the day. It could have lasted a century and he would have had enough sorrow to fill it. What gave him a sense of dread, of doom, was the day's immensity. The serene height and stillness of light tended towards doom. It brooded. Thick, heavy, and immobile, yet weightless, hovering, this immensity of light inflated the day almost beyond its limits of elasticity. Where he stood in the hall, Lear clutched the thickness of the wall and waited. One more second of the light's serene expansion, one stray fluttering among the shadows beneath the trees outside the window might catapult the day towards an explosion. Even twilight, when it came, would bring no relief. For twilight was like a slow explosion, something that, if it happened faster, would tear them all to pieces.

He heard Phillip Moravia moving about downstairs, the distant, almost musical sound of his human will and intelligence — books chafing against books as he handled them or moved them in stacks about the library, the hollow wooden ring as the top of his writing desk fell shut, the complex pattern of footfalls urged on by unknown thoughts and intents. Lear held his breath, praying. If Phillip Moravia came upstairs and found him in the hall and looked at him, the day would explode. It was best to remain hidden, suffer once more alone the haughty transformation of twilight — though before coming here he had had no idea how claustrophobic nighttime inside a house could be.

As the day grew so vast that it came apart, all the light fluttered up to the top of the sky while darkness thronged about the roots of things, anchoring them to the earth. He held an imaginary conversation with Phillip Moravia. He said:

Phillip Moravia, I am sorrow.

I am the looking out of windows by children with diseased brains who hear the dark room behind them rot and dread the morrow.

I am the dirt under people's houses that does not see daylight, collector of lost toys that roll there, beyond reach of the light.

I am the alley behind people's houses. Unpaved and overgrown, I don't go inside when it rains but lead away, always away — the road longing to follow itself, puddles open to the sky that looks down, down.

I am sorrow. You grew up in my house. Remember?

The house creaks loose from its moorings. The kitchen hangs from the trees, a wreckage held in a net of cockroach scurryings. A spoon dropping from the kitchen table drops to oblivion amid old tin cans and corpses clinking on the distant skin of the waters.

I am sorrow whole unto itself. By my desire my sorrow is halved and each half bleeds. Along the antique gutter sides of highways I walk, for sorrow walks on bones cast off from speed. Sorrow walks where the grass rusts, untouchable by events.

That house surrounded by dirt, yellow, gullied yellow in the light, so yellow one could not walk on it — see it with a pang — house surrounded by bare yellow dirt impassible — a stab in the eye. That was my house. In an upstairs bathroom the child sorrow stares into the mirror. He will not remember his childhood face, lost like the waters of the tub, a bath taken at the age of seven, hung from the limbs of that tree in a porcelain cradle held aloft by insects who hungered for his flesh as none has hungered since. He begged for beauty without knowing why, the child sorrow, while staring in the mirror. But he can't remember his childhood face.

I am sorrow. That was my house. The stair unravels. Bedrooms hang over the suckage of waters.

Remember in a dream once, something lost to the waters — the first whirlpool — a toilet flushed in fear, down, down into the cold plumbing of the house, irretrievable? And written above the mirror in rust — "Words of lust carved on a tomb are all you'll know of love."

The light was gone now. Lear darkened like a windowsill. Soon he would sneak down to the pantry to nibble scraps in some way least human — He'll just think he has rats, Lear told himself whenever he was driven to raid the pantry shelves.

And later in that lost bedroom he had chosen for the hiding of his sleep, when steeled with whiskey he stole from the cabinet downstairs his sorrow burned against sleep, he would stand before the mirror. A resignation would take hold of him with all the power of a defiance of horror and, slowly, he would take off his clothes.

Beneath the globe of the ceiling lamp that cast its light unwillingly on him, he viewed his nakedness mercilessly in the mirror.

Any attempt to arrange this lank threading of shell-like juttings and concavities into a pose that held some illusion of manliness created only an affected grimace of his skeleton, as though his body were prey to, ruled by some unnatural madness springing from his sex. Beneath his pitiless eyes his flesh unraveled and his eyes, dwelling on themselves, were a vengeance to themselves. He touched his lips with his fingers, afraid to touch himself anywhere else. And in the hypnosis of sorrow he spoke aloud. He said — "Phillip Moravia, I am sorrow. But I am more than sorrow. I am powerful.

"My love, why are you so solitary? Who or what do you desire? Is it yourself, perhaps? If I were you I would desire nothing but myself. But whomever you desire, whatever you desire, I am more powerful. For I know sorrow. I could love your corpse like the earth who would eat you slowly while telling you sweet lies to keep you from crying out until she had what she wanted. But I will see myself and live. I will flourish. My blood will give this ghost a voice."

This last word became a cry almost of doom. He fell away from the mirror onto the bed, which could only now receive him when he had had his fill of himself.

XIX

Inside the greenhouse the rain was deafening, but not a drop of rain fell. As he looked at the roaring walls of glass he felt the whole jungle, unmoored, rush upside down through the ocean toward some unnameable deep.

He found a spot beside a tree with low-lying, sinuous branches. The trunk sprang from the earth at a twisted angle, as though turning back in a frozen animal gesture. At its base steep phalanxes of root jutted into the earth.

He sat at the foot of the tree and, using his spade, buried his feet up to the juttings of his ankles in the black earth. Hugging the tree, he dragged himself up its trunk and wrapped his arms about the crook of a low-lying branch. He waited.

When he sensed the man enter the greenhouse, it was not so much a sight or a sound that warned him as the sudden consciousness of another human presence among the trees. Yet he had the terrifying sensation of someone who has snuck into a cage where a wild beast lies asleep and who stands prayerfully still, waiting to see what will happen when this beast awakens.

As the man approached it is possible he might have darted back into the shadows and remained unseen. Whether he did not uproot his feet through lack of strength or pure abandonment it would be hard to say.

When the man saw him, Lear looked him in the eye as directly as a wild thing looks into the eyes of that which has surprised it. Yet he was the one who lay in wait. He had never had such a consciousness of his own physical being as when this man's eyes first rested on him — both a wild hope for beauty and a hopeless realization of all the labor he must endure to return his body to the realm of the human. Even in his shame he could not look away. He looked at this man as though looking from out of his childhood, thinking both *Kill me* and *Be kind to me as though I were a child.* The man looked at him as though he were a ghost.

"I am a tree," Lear said. He then held out his hand.

His hand in the darkness was completely white, awesome in its fragility. It hung on the air as though, a thing he had let go of, it should have fallen.

The man stared at Lear for a moment. Then he sprang away and, spinning, clasped his arms round the trunk of another tree. He leant his forehead against the tree. He remained still, his back to Lear.

In the shadows, though only a few feet away, the man's figure cloaked by the dark fabric of his suit was barely discernible. Yet Lear could see the nape of his neck, could make out the rhythmic expansion and contraction of his flanks with the force of his breathing. Though Lear could hear nothing but the rain, this man's every breath looked so deep, so violent, he thought he should have heard it — in what way he did not know. As something hollow held by storms it called to him, though he could not hear it, could only guess it. This man's back was the most mysterious thing Lear had ever seen.

Having stood beneath that body, cowering in the hollow of his feet's burial, he now knew its height, could guess its girth and strength, could imagine himself walking towards that back and encircling it with his arms, his arms circling about those arms, holding them captive. While one hand crept up to lie against the nape of that neck, he would press his cheek against that breath-wracked back so that its heaving held against his ear would drown the rain. Closing his eyes he would fall into the hollow of that back where he would be held forever, as in a chamber more cradling than the rain, a chamber whose walls were washed by rains of blood.

He knew as clearly as he had ever known anything that the mystery of this man's back, in this moment and perhaps never again but for this moment, was his for the taking — that the arriving at this moment was but a prelude to the saving gesture he must make now that language had been routed and the strange storm he had unleashed in this man called to him.

Even as he knew this, he knew with a sickening certainty that he would not make this gesture, did not have the courage, and that the words he had spoken would work bitterly against him. Any tree could have longed less to embrace this man, to wrap him round with its branches, and moved forward to do so more easily than he, whose feet were rooted to the ground by the bitter knowledge that he would not make this gesture until it was too late.

He held out his arms. But as he looked at them he loathed them because he knew they only dared reach unseen, in the knowledge he would not step forward to let them find their mark. He was filled with the loathsomeness of the ineffectual and dropped his arms, knowing he would be despised.

The shame of his love came alive in him. The courage of his love, a moment before filling him to the brim of his lips and his questing fingertips with joyous intimacies, revelations, laughing secrets, scuttled backwards through a trap door in his soul and lost itself in his chill plumbing.

When the man turned round Lear did not dare look at him. He could barely stand. The man approached. He seemed to have collected himself. He looked down at Lear's feet, at where his ankles jutted from the earth. He crouched at Lear's feet and began clawing the black earth away from them. Lear held onto the tree with both his hands. He dared not look down. But he felt the exposure of his feet in the pit of earth. The man cleared the mud away from Lear's feet, digging with his fingers at the dirt between Lear's toes. Lear had soaked himself for hours in the lake and had carefully ripped off the gnarled curlings of his toenails. Beneath the mud his feet were white, cleaner than they had ever been.

The man rose. He rose up the length of Lear's body and towered over him. Lear cowered against the tree, his feet sunk into the pit of their exposure. The man stared down into Lear's face. Lear could feel the heat of his breath. Though powerful against his cheek, this man's breath felt, smelled to him like the suppression of something even more powerful — an animal hurricane held at bay, harsh insults and jeers perhaps, the breath, perhaps, of some inconceivable violence exhaling from those beloved nostrils, fanning from those lips, a violence no less a gift of this foreign life that towered over him than love exhaled. The man eyed his face as though waiting to see what his breath would do to it, as though hoping his breath would corrode Lear's face. He eyed Lear as though attempting to erase him.

"Who are you?"

Lear had never before heard the man's voice. And in this moment he almost hated its beauty, the power he could only have expected.

"Lear," he said. His name denounced him as he spoke it. "My name is Lear."

His own voice shocked him. Like a corpse dragged across stones, it made the sounds of a dead thing wantonly disturbed.

"You are no tree," the man said. "What do you want from me?"

Lear looked at his hands, waiting for them to speak. They kept apart from one another and from him. Every part of his body existed isolated in its shame. Yet within him was something that wanted to be known. His whole mute and hidden being was prey to a compulsion to make itself known to this man. His voice as he spoke was as painful to him as though through his mouth he gave birth to some living thing that would get out, though he could not prefigure its shape, tell whether it would be a thing of horror or of beauty. He did not care which, in his compulsion to be known.

"I have drifted away from humanity." His voice, the corpse dragged across stones, took back its life, stood and spoke. It spoke with the desolation of something dead and bewildered. "I have drifted away from humanity."

And then the man held out his hand through the forest, seized Lear's hand, pulled him forward — "That tree is poisonous. It could have paralyzed your lungs." And then he said with half a smile, his hand still holding Lear's oddly stiffly, as though in introduction — "My name is Phillip Moravia, director of the botanical gardens."

XX

That day when you followed him through the greenhouse into his laboratory, you had long ago passed into the zone of horror that was your love. He made you sit on the table. The exposed lightbulb above his head seemed natural to you in its hostility, his shape bending over you an eclipse in its glare, as though this were the clinical light in which you would always exist with him, a light created to illuminate his dismemberment of you. The rain on the tin roof was louder than madness. It would have absorbed your screams. You waited to scream, hungry for the knife.

His face as he spoke was forced up close to yours by the rain. "I must examine you. Please take off your shirt" — his voice emotionless yet commanding, as though it too held a knife. That was it. His voice held a knife to you, as did the sight of him.

So this was to be your nakedness before him — something abject and clinical, as though he would examine your wound. You hunched about your nakedness before throwing yourself open to the light. You lay back unfurled, unveiled, shame abandoned like an exploding blood clot in your throat. You closed your eyes, but through your eyelids you were covered by the blood of the light, the light a great eye covering you with the merciless blood of sight. You tried not to think of his eyes on you. You thought of his hands as the hands of the lightbulb handling you, holding you up to peer at. And yet you could not help thinking that even the lightbulb must be repulsed by you.

"You may dress," he said. You smiled before you opened your eyes — a smile forced on you by your triumph, for you heard the pity in his voice. This pity was like a kind of awe in which he held you, and therefore it was a triumph for you. You wondered later if he had seen your smile.

"You're lucky," he said. "That tree is called a Cleopatra Rossinensis. Its leaves are highly venomous."

And after a second — "But you are very thin. You must eat." And then, as if he could think of nothing else to say — "I'll get you something to eat."

Now that you were clothed once more you looked at him. Your eyes, carnivorous, delved into his eyes, snaked down into his hot and shadowy interior searching for his heart, which you would consume. It would be the only thing that would satisfy you.

Where you sat on the table your feet dangled above the earthen floor. You felt somehow as though you had just been created. And you looked at him, wishing he held this responsibility of creator toward you. Rows of wooden troughs supported by trestles stretched away in all directions. They burgeoned with vines and gave forth a dank smell of growth. These rows of vines contrasted oddly with the scientific equipment that skirted the room. This machinery, all of glass and cold metal, was foreign to you, and you did not try to fathom it.

"What do you want from me?"

You answered as truthfully as you dared. "I don't know... I don't know."

He watched you almost in fear. And you thought with a vengeful glory — *You think I am monstrous, don't you?* And out of your vengeful glory you smiled. But what you said was — "I can tell you things about the trees."

XXI

They dined in the library. Lear would not remember what they ate.

At the ringing of a bell, iron jangle hollowed by echoes from stone, he followed Phillip Moravia out into the hall and watched as he walked behind the upward sweeping of a stair to a narrow flight of stone steps leading down. Lear waited at the top as Phillip Moravia went down to open the door. As the door swung in, Lear recognized its outer face. He had passed by that door in his wanderings, had gazed at it with desire. Now as he looked down he saw Phillip Moravia silhouetted against the seething of the wet street. Lear's scalp crawled with the knowledge that he was inside, as though to be sheltered from the rain were the ultimate form of cold.

Outside a delivery boy stood beside his bicycle in the rain. His raincoat clung to the angles of his frame and accentuated the thinness, the almost forlorn tenderness of his limbs. Yet there was to this boy's stance a vigor, a virility that seemed to flow out of and to reenforce the frank and masculine structure of his face. The wet curls that clung to the solid symmetry of his brow were alive, snaking with virility.

And Lear thought with a pang that this boy could have been himself.

Phillip Moravia and the boy stood close to one another. Their hands touched, electrically to Lear's eye, as Phillip Moravia paid for the food. Lear watched with a strange jealousy the worlds that separated those two bodies as though they belonged to different yet complementary sexes. Then the door closed. The boy was gone. Phillip Moravia mounted the stairs and Lear was once more in the terrifying zone of his proximity.

Phillip Moravia served him some burning alcoholic brew from a decanter. In the candlelight Lear felt himself growing larger, bursting with secret power. For a while at least he gloried in his power. He gloried in the silence between them. He looked at Phillip Moravia and gloried in his power to look at him flagrantly.

But the silence grew too long between them. The room was in pain. They floated together in a dark unknowable space that opened outward from Lear's chest. The room was his chest and Phillip Moravia moved in the room like a knife. In the silence Lear heard the howling from his eyes as he looked at Phillip Moravia, a howling from the walls, his eyes a severed throat, mirrors severed on the walls. Horrified by his own eyes, he would have looked away but could not. Yet he did not look at Phillip Moravia. He looked at his throat, his shoulders, his hands. As Lear lifted his fork to his lips his wrists were severed in their shame. He looked down at his hands, wondering how most politely to lift them to his lips. And what would he do with them when he got them there? Would he eat his hands, as quietly, as politely as possible, whispering to them to hush if they cried out or tried to claw him in their pain?

The lower half of Phillip Moravia's body was hidden from him by the table. Yet he could see it with a horrifying clarity — not as though he visualized this unseen anatomy, nor as though he possessed X-ray vision and could see through the tabletop. He saw all of Phillip Moravia, both that half that was visible to him and that half that was not, as though he possessed two sets of eyes, one above the table and one below it, and both sets of eyes saw clearly and separately, both howled with an unspeakable desire. His eyes beneath the table saw as clearly as a cat's eyes in the dark every detail of the complex architecture of strain between those thighs and the chair on which they rested — the tautening of the dark trousers where the chair bit into the backs of Phillip Moravia's thighs, the strain where the thighs met and the sex was held disguised by a smooth curve of fabric. Here in this zone of great pressure diamonds and precious jewels were formed. In the horror of his desire Lear was hypnotized away from his shame, grew powerful in horror so that his eyes had the power to consume what they rested on.

Phillip Moravia's throat now lay on Lear's plate. This throat was not a fragment, something maimed, but a thing whole unto itself, reclining in the splendor of flesh cooked delicately in its own juices. Tenderly he ran the blunt tip of his knife along the ridge of muscle outlining the Adam's apple. Hollowing this niche, he raised the masculine swell of the Adam's apple to his lips and felt the secret quivering of heat and breath within it.

Slowly he consumed Phillip Moravia's throat. But vying with the throat for his attentions were the armpits, secret regions that do not need the incision of a knife to open onto the treasures within. And the armpits vied with one another, each opening onto a distinct and different world. He pried the left armpit open with his fingers as if opening a shell. He did not tear at the flesh but bore down along the muscles with a deliberate, prying pressure. The flesh opened of its own accord, released the dark embedded hollow that lay at the bottom of the flesh basin beneath wet rushes of hair. His mouth and eyes slipped down into this cave of secret hunger where tubular growths of hair, nippled tentacles, hung from the succulent vault.

No wonder Phillip Moravia looked so uncomfortable, at a complete loss for words. Lear watched him across the table. He reached to fill Lear's glass with brandy. Lear felt the burning of it in his throat as he watched the dark liquid spill from between Phillip Moravia's fingers.

Lear was beginning to get tipsy and considered taking a bite from Phillip Moravia's hand, but thought — "With the hands, later. Later it can be done with the hands."

He watched Phillip Moravia's lips move. From his distance he could not hear Phillip Moravia's words, could only read their shape. Phillip Moravia's voice was too in love with his lips to leave them. "How old are you?" Phillip Moravia's lips and right breast of a sudden lay on Lear's plate. As the lips spoke, they crawled up the outer swell of the breast. He saw Phillip Moravia's voice transformed into a hungering crawling of his lips across his own breast. Lear amused himself by making the lips suckle at the nipple for a few moments and then, growing jealous, ate them.

"How old are you?" The question spoken yet only seen hollowed the air. In the silence Lear saw himself sitting at the table, saw himself with a shock — the little boy still sitting in the train station. Lear waited for him to speak, finally to ask the time of a stranger.

He saw in the fragile length of that boy's limbs beneath his translucent skin a quickening of growth, a quick-slow eruption in the bone catapulting that boy's body towards the ghostly grown Lear who stood watching him. Time was desire, and was manifest in that boy's frame as a tangling of the bones in his chest, something ancient taken root in his bones and quickening them. Lear would have liked to register in that boy's eyes, speak to him, warn him of what he would become. But he could not. For he was still that boy. And the boy had always known in some strange way what he would become, that his destiny was longing. What he had not known was that longing itself can be wounded by finding its object. He could not force himself to speak or not to speak.

"What year is it?" he asked. Phillip Moravia seemed taken aback. But he spoke the date simply. The millennium, the century, the decade, the year rolled from his lips like a date of stone to stun Lear with the consciousness of his age. "Then I am twenty," he said. Seven years had somehow passed since his Mother had gone into the Ladies' Room. Though seven years seemed a long time, it did not seem so long as he might have dreaded or expected. He would not have been surprised to learn that he was an old man. Twenty seemed strangely full of hope to him. And this hope was an affront to him. It stung him with pity for his hopeless self. Were he alone he might have wept at the revelation of his age like an old man weeping over a life wasted by delusions.

"You had to calculate your age," said Phillip Moravia. "From what did you calculate — some event, some point in the past?" Lear could not answer. But suddenly he knew something he had not before allowed himself to realize — that he had avoided any knowledge of time's passage, had refused to allow himself to see the date, on the heading of a newspaper or stamped in the back of a library book. Had he realized what he was doing, this deliberate yet secret blinding, he would not have been able to stave off this knowledge for so long.

"Tell me about the trees," said Phillip Moravia.

Lear felt once more the terrible desire to be known.

"Talking comes hard," he said. "There is perhaps little to tell. I live in the park. I have been silent among the trees. At times I may have spoken, not in a whisper but not too much aloud either. Just in a voice, only as loud as a voice needs to be when speaking to itself. But most of the time I have been silent. At times I might have been moved to scream. Not out of any nameable emotion other than a desire to call out, to have my voice carry through the trees as the call of a bird does, or of some wild beast. One might think the birds call out to distance, to the sky itself, more than to one another. In such a way I would have called out among the trees. But I was afraid. Fear held me back. Fear of betraying my presence — but not so much to other human beings or to wild beasts. Betraying my presence to what then? I don't know. To something among the trees, I think. It comes in the night. It comes in terms of height. It comes from a great distance, from all directions. Yet it is already there and the distance rushes towards it. It gathers distance. The night gives this thing great power, so that in the dark it rushes towards visibility.

"It is as though all of life that is not human coalesces in the dark into a great and savage intelligence that raises itself up into the night. And I, in my solitary humanity, am filled with fear and awe before it. So that there has not been one night I have spent among the trees that I have not wound up cowering on the ground, curled in on myself, my head held in the hollow of my chest as though I hoped to turn my back into a shell wall to hold me and hide me.

"It seems to me that houses are built against this savage intelligence, and everything made by man is raised against it. But nothing escapes it. This savage intelligence imbues all things, and nothing made by man escapes it. Decay is part of this intelligence, its willful motion — so that at any moment I expect to see the houses move, transform themselves, just as I expect to see the trees move. Things are not inanimate. They wait. I can be still for a long time, in the same way that a tree is still —

as something that does not happen to be moving at the moment, though it may not have moved for a thousand years."

Phillip Moravia had risen from the table. He did not look at Lear, but off into the shadows. He moved slowly, randomly about the room. When Lear stopped speaking, he stopped — but he did not look back at Lear.

Lear had twisted round in the chair. His feet were twisted under him, his back hunched against the edge of the table. He crouched in the chair like a gargoyle. In the silence everything was suspended, immobile. He looked at Phillip Moravia. It seemed to him they were separated by a great expanse of night waters and that he struggled toward Phillip Moravia through the dark and terrifying deep. As he drew closer, Phillip Moravia loomed higher and higher until he realized that Phillip Moravia was a colossus rising up out of the deep. Lear clung to the black face of cloth veiling his thigh and tried to drag himself up it, as up a great black sail hung from the night sky. But the sail gave, as on a pulley, and sank beneath him, transforming into more of the dark water out of which he tried to climb. Lear shuddered, imagining himself drowned by the treadmill of the night sky.

Phillip Moravia spoke. His voice came up close to Lear and moved in the dark like a thing burdened by flesh. It lacked only the quality of visibility to be embraceable.

"As a botanist I travel a great deal. In fact, I am rarely here. I'm usually in some tropical region, looking for antique forms of vegetation, exotic plant life that has never been seen before. I don't go alone into the jungle at night. It's too dangerous. But I like to go off by myself during the day. It's one of my favorite things to do.

"In the jungle I have stood on a cliff and seen the green-scaled trees stretch out before me to a point where, stretching beyond the sun, they are too painful to look at and the distant light consumes them. Behind me in the camp, my guides wait — as far behind as I can have left them and still be back by sundown. My guides usually don't know the way anywhere except, remotely, the way back. You see, there is no destination to my journeys except deeper in — and what I find, I find by chance.

"As I advance I reach a point where it is as though a great chasm has opened up behind me. Before me the trees rise up in their power and shake their branches against the sky so that a metallic clamor showers from every leaf, and everywhere I look is something that would shine too brightly to be seen. I am dizzied and fall backwards into a blindness. My eyes flower. My brain bears branches, worshipful, all surface to the sky. I am comforted by the earth and beyond humanity.

"I know that at the root of my quest is something unnameable. Beyond this all else, the discovery and transmission of facts, the mechanism of research, the pushing back of the threshold of mystery before knowledge, is mere pretense."

Lear realized to his horror that he did not care what Phillip Moravia was saying. All conversation seemed to work against the flesh. His thoughts were hideous, disjointed, and he did not have the courage to think them or give them a name. From his remote corner of the room he could barely see Phillip Moravia. He saw himself. He saw his body hung on the air, a deceptive curtain covering a void. He saw that something ugly and shameful had burst through the wall of his chest and hung exposed on him, unrecognizable as a heart. It was the mouth of a wound grown ugly with desire for suckage, no longer able to conceal its emptiness. His longing was exposed to the air as a wrongdoing, his very flesh a wrongdoing hung on the air.

He saw his fingers uncoil from about the stem of his glass of brandy, saw the fear in his fingers, fear that they would betray him, fear that they might spill the glass, knock it from the table. And in mistrust of his every gesture he regretted not having spilled the glass, not having broken it. But it was too late. He had already let go of it. As always, the true gesture had escaped him.

He looked at himself with a strange dispassion and realized that he felt no desire for this flesh, no longing to inhabit it. He looked at himself with disinterested contempt, as he would look at the ugliness of a stranger.

As he looked, his eyes and brain leaked out, escaped the socket of his self and ran wild through the room, corroding the air that trapped the living flesh, restrained it, held it back from the horrifics of desire. In the darkness behind the corroded air he and Phillip Moravia stood and looked at one another. They were nothing but a pair of skeletons. As he had eaten of Phillip Moravia's flesh, secretly and politely at the table, so Phillip Moravia had eaten of his. They had picked one another to the bone and beyond, gullet having swallowed gullet. Even the entrails through which they had consumed one another were unraveled, gone. Not one strip of flesh was left twisting on a string of fat to arouse or revulse.

They looked at one another with their skull eyes, dark as the windows of upstairs rooms. Their mouths drawn wide with affectation held the skeleton of an unspeakable thought, something come unfleshed behind their grins long ago — for after all, what do skeletons have to say to one another?

Lear rushed towards himself from all directions, a hundred winds of Lear, winds of eyes that rushed into the dreaded crannies of his skull to inhabit it. Filled with a triumphant vengeance, his rib cage heaved, for he had never felt so dangerous, so happy in his skin as now when skinless, fleshless, he could flaunt his bones.

Desire was something in the air between these skeletons, as though the vacancy dangling below their boney groins were some bitter sap urging them on. The hollow sockets of Lear's eyes caught fire as he saw behind the darkness of the corroded air the machinery of desire grind up.

With a battle groan the skeletons flung themselves at one another. They wrestled. Driven by the air that longed for contact, for suction, for adherence, the skeletons struggled with one another. Jaw locked against jaw, nuzzling the comfortless bone. Rib cages tangled, interlocking, shuttling in and out of one another, shredding air.

Pronged bone thrust against bone, drawing shrieks of dry friction, wailings of scraped chalkboard. A hooked coccyx caught on the secret eye of a pelvic girdle and jerked against it, drawing from this orifice only dry, throatless scrapings.

Their hands groped and tangled in the chill of one another's bellies, searching for entrails to tug, to grasp. Hungry for the warmth of blood, of pain, they clawed up the chimney flues of one another's throats and bashed each other's skulls against the floor.

But in all the tangled, pronged heap of bones that lay between them they could not find one shred of flesh to use for love. There were no lips left on them, no dark interiors to fill, not one soft membrane to puncture or be punctured, no throat, no orifice, nothing that clasped or gave forth suckage, nothing to stab, nothing to stab with but the insensate bone. There was no bridge, no knife of flesh between them, only nerveless space clasped by two boney cages interlocking in a dry and sexless rape.

In the aftermath of their aborted love they recoiled from one another, struggling to disentangle one another's armatures. They sat spread-legged on the floor, groping about, searching their air-pierced bodies for the desire that was no longer manifest on them but drove them still. And they thought — "Where is it gone? Where is gone this flesh we could have used for love?"

But it was gone. They had picked it apart and eaten it, digested it discreetly and politely while the unspeakable thought had failed to disrupt the decorum of the meal.

They crawled about the floor like frantic dogs sniffing their discarded clothing, searching under furniture, sifting the debris of the table for one crumb, one scrap of flesh left between them that they might use for love.

And Lear laughed. As though through a crack in the wall his laughter came. He heard his laughter fill up the room, although he sat locked in silence, his limbs twisted around the chair, knotting him to it.

And Phillip Moravia did not suspect for one instant his hideous imaginings. Oh the horror of it, the idiocy, the waste! And he thought — "I am a monster. And you will not *escape* me, Phillip Moravia. You will not escape my monstrosity."

XXII

They were walking in the garden. Lear looked at Phillip Moravia in the night and thought — "Who are you? Who are you, this man that I so love? How dare you to exist?"

Phillip Moravia's silence demanded some explanation from him. He knew that Phillip Moravia waited for some explanation, though he did not look at Lear, looked away from him. Lear let Phillip Moravia walk a bit ahead of him, so he could see only his back. "I'll tell you a story," he said. Phillip Moravia stopped. Lear looked at the nape of his neck and the shell-like niche at the back of his ear, as though he would speak to these specific and, because specific, secret parts of Phillip Moravia. Imagining his words as his lips touching these places, out of his desire he was compelled to speak.

He said: "Once there was a little boy who lived with his Mother. They lived in a town far to the south of here, and their house floated on the waters. Whereas other people's houses stood on dry land, their house was adrift on giant mud puddles. For he and his Mother loved the rain so much the rain washed their house away from its foundations. The house and the two solitary creatures who lived in it were reflections of themselves in the waters.

"When he played in the backyard he drowned over and over. For even the earth in the backyard was drowning earth, and drowning was a great ecstasy to him. You can only drown alone. So he didn't play with other children, but drowned in the earth, drowned in the sky, drowned through his eyes, through his nostrils, through distance.

"His Mother encouraged him in his isolation because she had become convinced that she was not human and she didn't want him to become sullied by the humanity of other children. Then he might have begun to think that she was crazy. Whereas with no knowledge of the ways of others, everything she said and did seemed natural to him.

"Thus he was trained in the ways of solitary ecstasy.

"But his Mother began to hate the town where they lived. She feared old friends from her past, or relatives might try to visit. Her own mother might try to pay a call. So she took the boy away to a strange city in the North where no one knew them. They wound up here, in this town.

"As to what happened after that, the story could go in two different directions. It's possible the Mother told her son they were simply taking a vacation and that, at the end of the summer as they waited to catch the train back home, she abandoned him in the train station. He sat in the waiting room for seven years, waiting for her to come out of the Ladies' Room, afraid to go in and look for her. But I prefer to tell the story differently. I don't want to imagine it like that — though there is no denying that perhaps it was.

"I see rather that in their quest to transcend the drudgery of the flesh and all human contact, they wound up living in a place that had been long forgotten, long abandoned. I'm sure there are such places in this city — something like a forgotten cave... in a cemetery. They lived in this cave. I can imagine their life as though it really happened.

"Moving deeper into their solitary ecstasy, they were bit by bit surrounded, buried by the fetid, stinking bones life casts up — rot and decay stacking itself up around them as they flourished in their cave.

"Their life held something akin to murder at its core. Perhaps the way in which they fed secretly off of other people's lives to sustain the irreality of their own. In such a way he watched strangers with a perverse hunger.

"But they were not evil, he and his Mother, just practitioners of an eccentric asceticism, such as... people who try to be vampires, or to live off of the air itself, as trees do.

"In their secret life they became repositories for all that has fallen into decay, collectors of decay — and decay became beautiful to them.

"So much so that the little boy thought of himself as a ghost. When his Mother took him to the central post office to pick up their Social Security check, he would stand in the great marble hall, his body hung on the air like no more than a sheath, a translucent rag of flesh battered by the currents from the ceiling fans. He was so thin even the flies could not land on him. Nor did he sweat.

"His life was a constant withdrawal from the flesh. The corpses his Mother dragged home didn't seem strange to him. They were his friends. They sprouted as spontaneously as weeds from the walls of their cave. He didn't even wonder whether his Mother killed, or how she came by these corpses. Everything his Mother did seemed natural to him, and he was interested only in his own solitary ecstasy.

"We are different — we are artists," his Mother said.

"She said of the corpses — 'They are our anatomy lessons.' She would draw and paint all night long — corpses and skeletons, skeletons and corpses — gay, lively paintings, as though they were all at a party.

"His Mother only brought dead women home. Her tastes lay in that direction. 'The female nude,' she said, 'is where it's at! What can you do with a man's corpse? They were made more for battlefields. A woman's breasts lie so beautifully in death, still speaking, offering themselves for suckage.'

"Sometimes in the night she would go searching, importunate, for something she had lost in the hairy cleft between a dead woman's thighs. He would lie rigid in his bed, hardly daring to breathe, watching her. She would try to dig it out with a paint brush, or to snare it on the crook'd finger of a skeleton hand, this thing she sought — as though it were something looped that could be caught on a hook of bone. Sometimes she held a match to the lips of that fleshy cave and, puckering them, stared into that alluring refuge with one eye, her other eye all squinched, to see if anything were left alive in there. If she singed the hairy lips, she'd drop the match and wet the sex with her tongue to soothe it from its pain, whispering endearing words to it.

"With his fingers he counted his ribs compulsively, from one skeletal jutting to another, as though he were a ghostly pianist playing tunes on his own bones. In his bed he would raise his legs into the air and admire their hairless, waxen pallor. He thought of his own sex as a betrayal to his Mother. But at night in the secrecy of his bed, his hands would exhume his sex. Gazing at it as though it were the sex of another, he longed for it.

"He cast himself into the role of heroine in countless books. He read, one could say, to become a woman. All was love and sorrow for him, unattainable in life. To consummate his desires outside of a book would never have occurred to him. Outside of books, in his wanderings, what he sought was the inhuman. And he did not conceive of, hope for any communion with another.

"And then one day, he saw you through the walls of the greenhouse. And he loved you instantly. Perhaps not instantly. It's hard to imagine the fatal second before love takes place. But one would like to go back to it, that fatal second, and suffer the hideous transformation over and over — this boy like a ghost outside the glass watching you, with every second of his watching his frail being halved, translated into the horrific zone of love. What a wounding it was!

"Can you see him watching you through the glass, the trajectory of his life halted before you, his past stripped from him?

"His love froze him to the ground, and he couldn't go back to his Mother. His longing left no room in him for himself. If you look, you'll find his shoes buried in the spot where he stood and watched you. Apart from them there's nothing left of him — unless something taken root in his shoes has sprouted to reach for you from the trapped and twisted gropings of a tree."

Phillip Moravia had sunk onto the ground. He propped himself up with both his hands. Lear crouched behind him. He almost did not believe what he was doing. He reached forward and put one arm round Phillip Moravia's flank, lacing beneath his armpit so that he clasped the girth of his breast. He drew his other hand through the hollow between Phillip Moravia's neck and the hunched mass of his shoulder so that he cupped the side of Phillip Moravia's face. He laced his thumb round the delicate back of his ear. His fingers reached up along Phillip Moravia's temple into his hair. Slowly he began to kiss the back of Phillip Moravia's neck. Phillip Moravia remained still. He stopped clawing at the earth, and his shoulders grew less rigid. He arched his neck back, allowing Lear to travel round to the swell of his Adam's apple with his lips.

Then slowly Phillip Moravia rolled over onto his back and lay exposed to the night. His eyes were closed, his face a mask of pain.

In a thoughtless region Lear began to unbutton Phillip Moravia's shirt. Yet he could not stop thinking. He noticed how small and futile his hands looked undressing this glorious, strangely passive torso. He would have liked to rock and shake this great torso with his strength, lift it, knead it, reshape it into writhing gasps. But he knew in his awe and fear, almost a subservience before this strange, silent acceptance, that he would not have the strength. He noticed that his hands were too delicate in the unbuttoning of the shirt, that he should have ripped it open. He dragged the shirttail up out of Phillip Moravia's trousers. When the last button was undone Lear began to tremble. He felt he was about to unveil something too terrible to look at. He peeled the shirt and jacket back over Phillip Moravia's shoulders so that like bonds they restrained his arms, bound them to his sides.

Phillip Moravia's chest was revealed to the night. It was mysterious, massed from deep planes of strength. It was hollow and secret, and yet as massive and enduring as a trunk of stone.

Phillip Moravia's breath was exposed to the night. The rise and fall of that deep breast was painful to the eye. It placed Phillip Moravia in danger. The exposure of his breath was like the stripping naked of his precious life to the night.

Phillip Moravia had still not opened his eyes. His face was rigid. Lear looked at the slim, sculpted hollow where his abdomen crossed over, as across a dry river bed, into the region of his hip. From here down the zone of his sex was hidden, inviolate. He looked back at Phillip Moravia's lips. In the moonlight they were filled with intricate detail. Lear thought that if he wet those lips with his own they would remain hard and still and that the spittle of his kiss would lie in the sharp ravine between those lips like rainwater in the basin of an empty fountain.

Along the outer swell of Phillip Moravia's breast a sheen of sweat had broken — the sweat of hidden, quivering restraint. Lear knew that between Phillip Moravia's breast and his sex lay many miles. In the absence of any echoing passion, those miles were a mystery to Lear. His very life depended on the right crossing of this secret, breath-wracked landscape.

Lear wet his lips in the sheen of sweat along the outer swell of Phillip Moravia's right breast. Then he took the nipple with his lips. With one hand he cupped the rhythmic swell of the thorax. His other hand rested on the smooth, rounded heat of a shoulder. He tasted with his nostrils, with his lips, the passion of what he knew would not be. Assailed by a thousand odors of life, he was yet victim to a premonition of his own futility. Already his grip shriveled, his lips grew lax — knowing they were suckling at an impossibility, that they would be shaken off by simple lack of response.

Phillip Moravia sat up and cupped Lear's face with his hands for a moment. His eyes were terrible with pity, so far from desire as to be motherly. Then he stood. Lear was left crouching on the ground in a doglike posture.

It seemed to him in that moment that the fulfillment of some ancient doom had been enacted quietly — a doom not brutal but gentle with indifference as it brushed past him, almost failing to touch. The night did not need to pause one moment in its passage to reveal to him what would never be.

He felt the sand and earth torn from beneath his hands, from beneath his knees, torn from between the roots of the grass. But this was only his desire for some wave to take him and lift him, hurl him backwards into oblivion.

He looked down at his hands where the cold roots of the grass cut into them. The darkness gave a strange intimacy with his own flesh, so that his eyes and lips, his nose, loomed close up to the outcroppings of his limbs, nuzzling against them. Between his hands the pit of grass looked as distant and treacherous as an expanse of night waters seen from a great height. Strange to think that but a moment before a landscape of light had lain beneath him — a field of moonlit flesh. Like sorrow in dreams, light came from the flesh. Only flesh gave back any light from the darkness.

He looked up at Phillip Moravia. He stood with his back to Lear, buttoning his shirt. "Forgive me," said Phillip Moravia. "I shouldn't have let you do that."

Lear had been laid low by his desire. His shame quickened the night. It was outside of him now, running away. His shame looked just like a little boy to him. He crouched and watched this boy running away, already too far off, too late, out of earshot — no way to catch him, coax him back. It was a wild boy who would go on running. With the sudden knowledge that the present had already happened too long ago to salvage or to save, he realized that he would go on running with the wild impetus of lost things.

With this thought he suffered a strange widowhood. And the shame of his desire, laid open to the night, became an exaltation. His widowhood was imposed on him as a great and sorrowful dignity.

Where he crouched on the grass, no longer afraid to lift his head, it seemed to him he crouched atop a hill raised up as miraculous as an earthen throne. Phillip Moravia came up the hill now toward him as though climbing from a great depth. The slope was gentle, but behind this climber yawned a dark, vertiginous pull.

He stopped below Lear, and between them lay less distance than the length of a grave. They faced one another, the living so afraid to live that it seemed to Lear impatient hands might sprout from the earth to force them together. But the unfulfilled hunger of the dead can't force the living to brave life. Phillip Moravia spoke. "Don't you realize you're asking the impossible of me?"

They looked at one another. There is not much to say to atone for our acceptance of the fact that we were made for tragedy, not love.

They walked back toward the house. Humbled, Lear yet felt the pride of tragedy, some harsh, pinnacled architecture, erecting itself within him.

XXIII

As he lay in that room besmirching the solitary bed, the pride of his monstrosity came back to him, a thing unsought yet unavoidable in the night.

He got up and looked in the mirror. In the moonlight his eyes were two separate intelligences conjoined within his face by a common knowledge of cruel intent. He went downstairs.

As he lowered the great drop leaf of the desk he wondered what secret, calculating chamber of his brain had tricked him into remembering, into noticing where the money was kept. It lay in the dark behind Phillip Moravia's manuscript. Lear reached beyond the manuscript, fearful of brushing against it. As he feared, he touched it.

Lear took one page from the manuscript and wrapped the money in it. This piece of paper stolen at random, the first word on it perhaps not the beginning of a thought, the last word dangling over the void from which it had been stolen, the words not words to him but pictures of his love — would be the only memento of Phillip Moravia he would take. The money it contained — all the money he had found — was the quantity of his future. He had no conception of how much of a life could be symbolized by such a sum, nor did he care. He did not count it.

Moving through the library, through the laboratory, through the greenhouse, he found the pane of glass he had loosened with his spade. He crawled outside. Beneath the boxwood, he could feel the stirring of the night, its restlessness. He dug with his spade, hoping he would strike some inconceivable root. But when he unearthed his shoes he found that nothing had sprouted from them. He left that house.

Crawling out from the boxwood, he found himself in a part of the garden he had never seen. Before him two stone walls of great height ran away into the night, parallel to one another. They enclosed a narrow isthmus, a secret road of grass. He followed this road. The grass was deep as wading shallows and stirred in the nagging wind. He came to a place where a hedge of great height ran from wall to wall, masking what lay beyond.

Beyond the hedge a single tree of enormous height rose up into the sky. The tree was massive, old. Many of its lower branches were dead. But the great central crest still flourished. He could hear the sighing of the boughs, could see the dark crest stir like black flame against the sky.

He hoped that beyond that great tree the walled road would lead on forever, toward some place he could not conceive of. He moved forward, but before he reached the hedge he stopped. He could not bring himself to penetrate beyond that wall of leaves, not yet. He veered and huddled against the wall. He waited. The wind rode down, tugging at things, searching. Up in the sky two torn white clouds rode past like empty platforms.

The wall of leaves parted. Phillip Moravia stood in the grass before him. He was naked. The grass swayed against his thighs. The flesh of his torso, of his shoulders and his thighs was crossed by thin wet lacerations. Here and there blood still blinked in them. His sex was like a clenched fist. From it a pearled strand dangled, some elastic aftermath gone unnoticed in his abandon. Lear pressed himself against the wall, hiding from this man he had never known, this man unknowable.

Phillip Moravia's head swiveled from side to side. His glance swept the open expanse of grass. His eyes grazed the surface of Lear's eyes. Though they did not register him in the shadows, Lear wondered why their passage had not killed him.

Phillip Moravia moved forward, parting the grass. The strand of semen dangling from his sex was slung off and lost in the night, a silver arc. When he reached the farther hedge of boxwood, he thrust his body into it without raising his hands to part the branches.

Lear leaned against the wall, alone in the grass. After a while he thrust himself into the wall of leaves from which Phillip Moravia had appeared, taking no care, deliberately letting the branches cut him. On the other side he saw the road of stone ended. The two walls met, became a single wall circling back on itself. This, then, was the end of the garden.

At the center of this semicircle of stone the tree reared itself, a tower into the sky. At the roots a dark patch of wet shone. He touched the dark wetness and, drawing away his hand, saw that it was blood — Phillip Moravia's blood on his hand. He sank to the ground and tried to imagine what inhuman desire to embrace had caused this man to wound his flesh against the bark of the tree.

He licked the blood from his hand. Then kneeling, he crawled about among the roots, around and around the tree many times, his knees on fire from his crawling — trying to search out some trace, some little drop of the white liquid he knew must have been spilled there. But in all the intricacies of black dirt and root he found nothing. He laid his head against the earth for a moment and closed his eyes, knowing that the earth had betrayed him. Then he left that place.

XXIV

He bought a ticket somewhere to the South, towards that town whose name he dared not pronounce, almost hoping it no longer existed.

Behind him, out the great portal of the train station, dawn waited on the sidewalk, setting down old suitcases. He walked to the door of the waiting room and looked across at the bench where he had sat. Beside it in the shadows the night janitor was emptying his pail into a bower of ivy after having mopped the floor. He wiped his brow with his sleeve, then rolled the bucket away, steering with the mop handle as though sailing a small boat across the sea of reflections. Lear walked up to the mass of ivy and, thrusting the leaves apart, saw that it did not spring from an urn but from his ancestral luggage which had rotted, fecundated, and taken root in the floor. He looked at the stone warriors above him. He thought of his Mother traveling north by train with this strange, unknowable little boy — up the seaboard to take their summer in a cheap hotel in this city which was as far north as she would ever dare go. And for the first time it occurred to him to think it strange that they had never had any other living relatives.

The train station began to fill up with life. A group of well-hatted old ladies up early for a pleasure excursion were discussing cancer operations near the door. A lovely little girl decked out in lace grew enraged because her mother would not buy her a piece of chocolate cake from the pastry concession. She grew red, as though her face were about to explode, and had to be physically restrained. Three black children of staggered sizes holding hands in a row watched her. Their eyes grew wide with awe, and their parents could not get them to move until the little girl had been carried away.

Lear felt a defiant joy, as though he were a walking instrument of magic. In the men's room a businessman with a briefcase and a bearded bohemian gentleman stood side by side at the urinal, toying with their sexes and eyeing one another. Watching them, Lear was comforted by the heroic perversity of men.

In the afternoon he boarded the train. He brought with him a provision of sandwiches and wine, which it had taken him hours to gather up the courage to buy. But he did not begin drinking until after sunset, and only much later, when his hunger was overpowering, did he eat, feeling a strange shame as though food did not accord with his exaltation.

Most of the passengers were black, imbued with a strange Southern innocence, an innocence people sometimes attribute to the past. The festive spirit of travel, a childish excitation at distance and departure, pervaded the car. As the train bore into the night, everyone was hushed, lulled into sleep by its rhythm, trusting in their sleep.

Through the window of the darkened car Lear watched the land passing in the night. His eyes were shadowed caves held before him in the glass. He peered through his eyes as though he were the ghost of the landscape peering in at himself.

The night lay across the land in great distances, fanning the land past from the one remote, still point that kept abreast of them. The moon followed the train. At times the line of trees rushed up to the window. The branches strained toward his face. Then they were torn away. The line of trees zoomed back in a dwindling flight — a crazed black ribbon of spikes behind barren fields. The black ridged earth of the fields swoll like vast water — drowning earth. Farmhouses containing themselves against the wash of the fields were arks of sorrow. Towns were sorrow — decay and ancience trapped in the web of their outskirts, drifting wreckage of land

and time caught in the net of the streets. As they moved deeper South the towns grew humbler, their hold on the earth undermined by the crazed vitality of the surrounding vegetation. The towns were made of sorrow, the landscape unattainable.

At times moored in a station, the passengers grew restless, frightened awake by the train's stillness. The iron awnings of the quays which had drifted up around them now held them in the sweet night air of that town's particular sorrow — the smell of it drifting in through the open doors of the carriage. He looked out at streets traveling away between stone flanks of bank buildings and high brick façades of dark hotels, all older in the night than pyramids and built according to a purpose more obscure — billboards, dead neon signs of liquor stores, antique advertisements rotting off the walls of filling stations — the streets wet with a rain that had passed away before them, the weather always traveling ahead of them or away from them — that town's particular sorrow reflected in its wet streets.

Then the train began to roll again. The streets slid away and they were once more held by the passage of the land. He was borne across the night outside the train like something wounded against the broad passage of the earth — his chest dragged across ridges of stone and dirt, lacerated by the rushing crests of trees.

He remembered himself as a child on this very train, this Silver Meteor, heading North or heading South, he couldn't remember which. Nor could he remember his age — a year somewhere before desire. He had looked down the aisle in the night and seen asleep in one of the train's deep seats a man more beautiful than any he had ever seen. Lear loved him instantly. He could not now guess that man's age, having then no inkling of a span of years separating him from what he did not know he would become. The man was probably no more than twenty. To Lear he was a god. And Lear loved him, accepting the impossibility of that love for reasons other than he would now. Yet the love had been no different, the same miraculous wounding.

Sometime after dawn the train stopped at his town. The forest was so thick here the mist had not yet risen. He got off the train. There was no sign of the town from here, only a road that led inland, away from the station. The town had drifted deeper into the wilderness, unlike most towns that drift away from it. Other passengers got off and drove away with friends or relatives. The taxis gave up waiting. When there was no one left he moved out from beneath the eaves of the station and began to walk.

On either side of the road banks of weeds burned and hissed beneath the mounting brilliance of the day. Scrub pines kept abreast of him. He was filled with fear that the ecstasy would be lacking. But this fear was a form of ecstasy.

He came to the outskirts where the trees fell away behind great dunes of white earth. Everywhere, stalks of weeds hissed and chattered. Beyond more railroad tracks, at a conjoining of roads, the city dump was held aslant a broad swell that rose toward the back of the cemetery. Beyond the cemetery, thick with trees on the distant ridge, he saw the steepled curve of the town. The vast ashen slope of the dump sparkled in patches of encrusted foam. Gulls circled and swooped to forage in the glittering crust. Buzzards wheeled away to the west, inland over the pine forests.

He mounted toward the ridge of the town. Its rooftops were held in a huge bouquet of oak leaves. The sand beside the road was fine and white, and rose in a bone dust behind him. Burnished stalks of weeds clattered as he brushed against them.

As he entered the shadow of the town he was held by a cool smell of rot that hovered about its baseboards and breathed out from cellar windows and from under porches. Few people were abroad at that hour. Those who were moved slowly, hypnotized by the density of light. The season had retreated. Summer still held sway here.

The Negroes were the only ones who did not hug the shadows. They walked in the sun and did not look at him. They seemed always to be moving away, around blinding street corners, or down long stretches of street that ran into the sun, so that even the wood floors of the porches were bleached grey by the light. They moved slowly into the dust of light held above their unknowable backs.

The few white people he saw were all old ladies. They descended from the shadow of vast porches to water the roses or perform some other ritual task that he imagined must consume their days. Shutting off their hoses, they retreated behind screened porches, behind screened doors and windows to continue the wrapping of themselves in silk through the afternoon.

Children raced through the hollowed hearts of parks, gone mad inside the day's huge aviary of sky and jungle gyms, of shrieking swings and dirt. He skirted the parks, hoping to avoid the children. But sometimes, out of cruel instinct, the children spotted him, smelled him in the distance. The echo of their savagery was stilled, quieted for a moment. And through the hall of trees their piercing eyes telescoped to him their sudden knowledge of him. All eyes turned towards him, the distant bodies frozen in the game, telescoping to him their sudden cruel knowledge of him. Quickly, he turned a corner, hoping the children would forget what they had seen.

He moved deeper into the shadow of the town, trying to feel out with his feet on the bricks and pavements where, through the rotting streets, his house had drifted.

The neighborhood grew poorer, the houses vaster. Rot shifted up from the foundations into the eaves, climbed from the branches onto the rooftops. Through the downward drifting of its inhabitants, this neighborhood of Victorian streets had achieved its final blossoming into eccentricity. The air continued the architecture — a jeweled curtain dangling from the trees — a screen of broken toys and bottles, birdcages, rain-washed laundry. Children with disconnected eyes played stubbornly in the dirt of front yards. Their skin was whiter than fungus beneath sheaths of dust caught from their diggings in the grassless dirt. They played shiftily. Sullen, they would have refused to notice him. But he was already followed by a gang of other children, a pack of vicious brats whose numbers grew with each park he passed. Unable to resist the smell of a common victim, they straggled along behind him. Hushed by malign curiosity, they kept their distance. Yet he felt their urge to overtake him, fell him, swarm over him, and trample him into the dirt. They wanted to pick him apart and beyond, to fight over his bones. Their bare feet beat the clay of vacant lots and the dusty skin of the pavement like a drumroll beating out behind him — "Death!

Death! Death by children!" The pack magnetized more followers, even from among these sullen brats with inward-turning eyes, suspicious of all their fellows. He advanced slowly, looking for his house, knowing one false move would cause the pack to swarm up over him.

The houses withdrew as he approached. Slow-watching eyes at the windows sank back into the darkness behind the screens, not wanting to witness, to attract the massed savagery of the children. They followed him across a railroad track and into an open bowl of cornfield. On the white dirt road that ran across this field the children faltered, sensing their distance from him dwarfed by the surrounding emptiness. They followed him onto the black side of town.

Here the buildings were lower, porchless — tin-roofed wooden boxes that hugged the streets. Here and there a crude balcony jutted from a second storey, casting a coffin-shaped shadow on the sidewalk. The trees were all out back of the houses and raised their branches in shadeless silhouettes over the burning rooftops. Wheelless cars sank into the dirt. The Negro children, frozen for a moment in the day's heat, watched him pass. But they did not join in the gang that followed him. Inscrutable, partaking in this savagery only with their eyes, they had learned too well whose sacrificial rites they should not witness.

The streets grew more barren. The houses were unbroken lines of wooden walls fronting the streets. He began to walk faster, hurried on by the streets toward the distant point at which they were funneled into the throat of the light.

Beyond this throat, at the most barren, light-bleached outskirts, beyond the ice warehouses and the tongue of salt marsh, other streets, the drifting streets, received him. These were lost streets, oppressed by grappling trees, oppressed by shade. An unknowable smell, a flowering rot held the streets in emptiness like the ghost of a rabid dog. He could tell that no one had been outside in some time. This was the ancestral neighborhood where his house had drifted in its shame. Behind him the children shuddered and moved closer to one another. They smelled through the thickening air a nostalgia so potent as to erase them. When he stopped before his house the children fell back in fear, knowing of a sudden who he was.

The house stood in a forbidden zone. Even the fiercest bully, under solemn dares, wouldn't go near it. Lear walked up onto the porch and touched the glass knob of the door. Behind him a rumor of wonder and of awe rose up from the children. He turned the knob and went inside.

As he passed into that dark he knew in his perversity that he would make the children wait for years, until they were a gang of skeletons waiting out front of his house, but they would never know what had happened to him. He didn't want to give them that satisfaction.

Inside the house the rooms waited. Upstairs and downstairs the rooms waited. The looking out of windows waited. The staircase waited in its dank century. And yet he had the impression that nothing awaited him in that house. All memory was but an odor. Nothing was left but a smell, and that smell maddening in its lack of power to drag him back through time.

He could not tell from what the sweetness of this smell was made — something only a moth could thrive on. Yet he once had thought it might sustain him. It lured him into corners where he huddled against the walls, his soul gone weeping, trying to let himself be dragged back by the nose through time. He could crouch here through a whole day and the light's familiar fanning down from gold into the tall dislocations of the night. But he knew that in the dark he would grow too frightened. This was not a place to come back to except in dreams.

There was only one place left to look. He moved through the shadows of the house toward the back door. The slamming of the screen stabbed with the keen point of perfect memory. Startled crows wheeled from the treetops. Their cries came back twice, echoing in the backwash of their departure. He was left with nothing but the trees and dirt. At the back of the yard was a screen of weeds and vines, the point of mystery, the place where he had been lured toward death so many times.

"I'll stay outside and play till all the moths in a night have been burnt up," he thought.

He began to wheel around and around with his arms outstretched, slowly at first, then faster, faster — forcing himself to the speed of pure abandon. He strained for the point at which his eyes and brain, his arms would be cast off. An old lady saw him from her distant window and, at first, thought he was just playing. The trees whirled round him, a jagged fence of spikes. The house whirled round him, eyeless in its speed. He laughed from the center of his explosion.

But before he reached the point of his destruction he was felled, tripped backwards by a stone. He rolled across the earth. The trees fell down on top of him. The sky rushed past him, down, down into the belly of the dirt. He heard the earth jabbering of mudpies and of ziggurats, and the sweet flavor of our flesh. The earth crooned in its gluttony. But just before it swallowed him, some horrible fear of drowning made him struggle. He clawed his way up out of the open breach.

When he had reached the verge of his escape, when just within reach of solid ground he might have clung to it for safety, he realized of a sudden how horribly his instinct to survive had betrayed him. Wailing, he flung himself backwards into the earth. But it was too late. The breach had closed. All that was left of that abyss he had so longed for were a few gashes he had made with his spade in the dirt.

He stood and looked around him. Each seeing of the trees, each seeing of the sky, was a seeing of these things a thousand times. Incredible how the light, the distance called to him. Behind him the roof of the house had fallen open. Through the yawning eaves vines and bracken clenched the bedsteads. Branches twisted through the windows. The bathtub had burst through the sagging of the wall below an upstairs window and dangled on the brink. Its curve, choked with rotting leaves and stagnant water, resembled a strange smile. The trees splintered the house and upheld it. The odors of the earth upheld all things.

He was lashed to life. His longing was slung round the earth a thousand times. And he set off following it. He did not know where he was going. •